THE BLACKSTONE SHE-BEAR

ALSO BY ALICIA MONTGOMERY

The True Mates Series

Fated Mates
Blood Moon
Romancing the Alpha
Witch's Mate
Taming the Beast
Tempted by the Wolf

The Lone Wolf Defenders Series

Killian's Secret
Loving Quinn
All for Connor

The Blackstone Mountain Series

The Blackstone Dragon Heir
The Blackstone Bad Dragon
The Blackstone Bear
The Blackstone Wolf
The Blackstone Lion

The Blackstone She-Wolf

The Blackstone She-Bear

To Lauren

Your golden rejoining will bring to life something even more beautiful.

I look forward to Version Eight.

This is a work of fiction. Names, characters, businesses, places, events, locales, and incidents are either the products of the author's imagination or used in a fictitious manner. Any resemblance to actual persons, living or dead, or actual events is purely coincidental.

Copyright © 2018 Alicia Montgomery
Cover design by Melody Simmons
Edited by LaVerne Clark

All rights reserved.

THE BLACKSTONE SHE-BEAR
BLACKSTONE MOUNTAIN BOOK 7

ALICIA MONTGOMERY

PROLOGUE

Four years ago

Mason Grimes wrestled with his inner animal, attempting to calm the beast down as he entered through the doors of The Den. *For fuck's sake, it's only a bar.*

Fucked-up animal that it was, his polar bear was calmer right before a dangerous op than in social situations. And, since he was a Navy SEAL, dangerous didn't even begin to describe all the shit he'd been through in the last nine years.

But then again, this wasn't an ordinary bar. This was a bar that catered to other shifters, and all the different energies in the enclosed space made his animal agitated.

He swallowed a snarl when another patron—wolf, based on the stench of wet dog—got too close to him. When he spotted Tim from across the room, he breathed a sigh of relief. His uncle was a good man; gruff on the outside, but when things got rough at home, he was the only one who stepped up.

Tim must have felt his stare, because his head whipped toward him. Much like Mason, Tim was a large man, over six foot five and sported a beard, but his hair was completely white. He looked like an older version of Mason, which made sense of course, because Tim was his dad's older brother.

Light blue eyes—also like his own—stared back at him. Surprise flickered across Tim's face, just for a moment, but by the time Mason reached the bar, the other man had his usual stoic expression on his face.

"Well, boy, nice of you to drop by after all this time." Tim crossed his arms across his chest, and the red flannel shirt he wore strained against his biceps.

Mason laughed. "Thought you might need your diaper changed, ya old fart."

Tim's snowy brows furrowed together. "You volunteerin'?"

"Hell no! I was going to laugh in your face, then get the hell out when you stunk up the room."

His uncle's face remained stone-still for a second before he did something rare. His head went back and let out a loud belly laugh. It startled the people around them, including the young man working the bar whose eyes darted nervously from Tim to Mason and back again.

"Come here, you runt." Tim grabbed his arm, his meaty hand wrapping around Mason's elbow.

"I haven't been a runt since before my growth spurt at seventeen." Mason returned the gesture and pulled his uncle closer so they could touch their foreheads in the traditional greeting for polar bears. No one dared make a comment, nor did Mason feel weird doing that in front of a whole room of people. After all, he and Tim were the last of their family, and possibly their kind. As far as he knew, there were no other polar bears around, at least not in this part of the world.

"So," Tim began when he pulled away, "what brings you to Blackstone?"

"I wanted to see you."

"Me?" Tim huffed. "It's been nearly a decade since you left and joined the SEALs. I know what kind of shit they put you through, so I'm not complainin'. I still get your letters, though. Damn proud of you, boy."

"I got more news. Good news."

"Oh yeah?"

Mason nodded. "Got promoted and I'm leading my own unit. It's a brand new one. Shifter Team Six. An all-shifter team."

After decades, it seemed the navy had finally seen the potential for the use of shifters in their operations. After all, shifters were stronger and faster than normal humans, not to mention being able to turn into different animals had a distinct advantage. It was a wonder it took them so long to figure out that shifters could be useful in covert ops, but then again, the human world wasn't exactly welcoming of their kind.

"You gonna be leading your own team now?" For the second time that night, Tim did another rare thing—he actually smiled. "I didn't think I could be any prouder of you. You know your old man would be shitting his pants with happiness if he were here, right?"

Mason managed to smile back, despite the tightening in his throat. "Yeah."

Tim clapped him on the shoulder. "We should celebrate. The usual?"

He nodded and Tim wasted no time getting behind the bar. As owner of The Den, no one stopped him, of course. He reached for shelf behind him for three beer glasses, filled each one from the tap, and brought them over to where Mason was standing. He slid one glass over to Mason, kept the second in front of him, and the third next to the empty spot beside him. For your dad, he would always say. "Congratulations."

"Thanks." He clinked his glass to Tim's and they both took a healthy swig before slamming the glasses down on the bar. Mason's eyes darted to the untouched glass before looking at his uncle. "So, what's new, Tim?"

"Not much since you left. Same old, same old. And"—Tim's face went back its usual scowl when a loud crash interrupted him—"speaking of which ..."

"Go ahead," Mason said, taking another sip of beer. "I'll be here. We can catch up later."

"Right. You got a place to stay?"

"I'm fine. Just checked into the Blackstone Motel off 79."

Tim grunted then turned, walking out from behind the bar and toward the source of the commotion.

Mason shook his head. Though nine years had passed since those couple of months he'd spent in Blackstone, Tim hadn't changed one bit. He glanced up at the mirror behind the bar, inspecting his own reflection. With his thick ruddy beard, broad shoulders, and the hardened expression in his eyes, he was certainly far from the tall, skinny seventeen-year-old who had arrived in Blackstone all those years ago.

He remembered his dad, before he died, telling him about his brother in Blackstone, Colorado. Mason hitchhiked and walked all the way there, then asked around until he found Tim. Despite the fact they had never met, the old man recognized him right away and offered him a place to stay. He'd only stayed in town for a couple weeks until he was old enough to enlist. Even when he was younger, he knew he wanted to be a SEAL, just like his dad. If only his old man was around now.

He took another swig of beer, pushing the memories away as he swallowed the bitterness down, along with the cool liquid. He turned around slowly, trying to settle his bear before facing the entire room of shifters.

Mason prepared for the inner battle, but to his surprise, his animal went silent. In fact, the entire room went still; the people, the bar—everything blurred away in his vision. Except for *her*.

He couldn't look away, and for a moment he forgot to breathe. She had just entered the bar and was standing in the doorway, her head turning side to side, as if looking for someone. Even from a distance, he knew she was quite possibly the most gorgeous woman he'd ever seen. Tall, with long, dark blonde hair going down her back. She was wearing a black leather off-the-shoulder top and skintight jeans that showed off her generous curves. He'd had his share of women in the past, but for the life of him, couldn't recall a single time he'd wanted someone this *bad*.

Mason put his beer down and dropped a tip on the bar before he began to make his way across the room. It seemed she'd found her companions, as she began to walk toward one of the tables in the far corner. His bear growled, as if urging him to go faster before she got away. *Hold your horses. She's not getting away from me.*

As he walked after her, his eyes zeroed in on her ass. Full and shapely, and he could already imagine grabbing it as he—

He stifled a groan, and focused on his task. *Can't let her get away.* His hand stretched out to catch her arm, and as their skin touched, a strange warm feeling crept over him.

She turned, her hair whipping back. Blue eyes, the color of

the sky after a rainstorm, crashed into his. Pink, plump lips parted and sucked in a breath as he heard a loud roar from within him

Mine!

Now that was strange. His polar bear never talked with actual words. And as far as he knew, no shifter's animal did. But then again, he grew up in a small, backwater town in Tennessee, and there were no other shifters there. In fact, he'd never met one until Tim.

Mine, his bear insisted, roaring loudly in his ears.

And, much to his surprise, he could feel *her* animal shout it at him, too.

Mason staggered back. *Holy hell.* He could smell the fur and something else—sweet, like honeysuckle. A female bear. Grizzly. And not just an ordinary one. There was something different about her. Something fierce and loud and magnificent.

Her eyes remained fixed on him, and she was still as a rock. Up close, she was even more beautiful, and in her high heels, she was only two or three inches shorter than him. *Shit.* Long legs, curvy ass, full tits. He was a goner.

Finally, she spoke. "Oh. It's you?"

He frowned. No way they'd met before. He would have remembered. "Do I know you?"

She blinked. "I mean. They always told me ..." She cocked her head to the side and her eyes narrowed. "Maybe it's not you."

"I'll be whoever you want me to be, darlin'," he drawled. "What's your name?"

"Amelia. Walker."

"Beautiful name."

Her face went all pink and her eyes lowered, her full lashes casting shadows over her high cheekbones. Based on what she was wearing, he would have thought she was some rocker, man-eating chick. But, she seemed almost sweet. Maybe a little shy.

"I'm Mason Grimes. You here alone?"

"No." She nodded her head toward two girls who were standing around a table in the corner. "It's my friend Kate's birthday. She just turned twenty-one."

"Nice," he said. "I'm not from around here and I don't know anyone. Maybe I can join you guys for a bit, Amelia?"

"I—" Her eyes dropped to his hand, still wrapped around her arm. "I don't know. I mean, I don't know you and my friends might—"

"I'm Tim's nephew," he said. "You know him, right?"

"Oh." She glanced over at Tim, who was back by the bar. "Then in that case—"

"Let's go meet your friends."

Amelia nodded and gently tugged her arm away. His bear didn't like that, and growled, but he tamped it down before it screwed things up. She frowned, and much to his surprise, her bear protested as well. He could feel it roar, but it backed down as she reined it in with practiced ease. Fuck, a woman in control like that was hot and he wondered what else she was good at.

He followed behind, not caring if he looked like a damn puppy chasing after her. She stopped at one of the tables, where the two women were waiting.

"Finally," one of them said. "You're here and you wore the outfit!" The two other women were wearing the same leather top and jeans. "We've been—" Green eyes turned to Mason. "Jesus H. Christ on a bicycle! Where the hell did *you* come from?"

The young woman's glance was appreciative, her eyes devouring him from top to bottom. He wasn't stupid; he knew women found him attractive, and this one was cute. But right now, his focus was on one particular woman. When Amelia stepped in front of her friend, he swore he could feel her bear's hackles rise. The possessive move was hot and only made him want her more.

"He's Tim's nephew," Amelia explained.

"Whoa, cowgirl!" The woman threw her hands up. "I'll try not to get too close, yeah?"

Amelia glanced around and gave Mason an apologetic look. "Sorry, I don't know ... I mean ..." She shook her head. "Mason Grimes, this is my friend, Kate Caldwell. She's the birthday girl."

"Happy birthday, Kate," he greeted with a nod.

Kate looked at Amelia warily before extending her hand. "Nice to meet you, Mason."

He shook it, surprised at her strength despite her slight frame. Shifter, of course; wolf or maybe coyote, he guessed, from the scent of fur.

"And this is Sybil." Amelia nodded to the other woman who had walked over to him.

"Mason Grimes," he said as he waited for Sybil to offer her hand.

"Sybil Lennox." She was petite and curvy, with sparkling gray eyes. A pretty little thing, really. But when he shook her hand, his bear reeled back in a defensive position at what he felt was a large, tightly-coiled creature inside her. He couldn't smell fur or feathers, and he'd never encountered anything like it. Though he wanted to ask her what she was, shifter etiquette made him bite his tongue.

"Are you visiting Tim?" Sybil asked.

"Yeah, just here on leave," Mason answered. "They're shipping me off again in two weeks."

"Army?" Kate interjected.

Mason shook his head. "Navy. SEALs."

"Ooohhh!" Kate clapped her hands together. "Sounds dangerous!"

He shrugged. "I suppose. But I'm still here." He really hoped they wouldn't ask about his missions. Not only were they classified, but the things he'd seen … it was a good thing his bear was already messed up before he'd even enlisted.

"Mason?" Amelia had placed a hand on his arm and she looked up at him with concern in her eyes, her soft palm warm on his bare skin. "Are you all right?"

"I'm fine." Her touch was oddly soothing. "So," he said, turning to Kate. "You just turned twenty-one?"

Kate's face lit up like a firework. "Oh yeah. I'm legal, baby. Legal to drink, anyway."

Sybil snorted. "You've been sneaking gin from your dad's liquor cabinet since you were seventeen."

"Yeah, well it just means I can get a drink anytime I want now." Kate raised a fist in victory.

"Speaking of which," Mason began. "Since it *is* your birthday and I invited myself over, maybe I should buy you a drink?" He glanced at Amelia. "I mean, all of you?"

"Free drinks? Woohoo! You bet!" Kate slapped him on the shoulder. "A shot of tequila!"

"And you ladies?"

"Just a glass of red," Sybil said.

"A beer," Amelia added. "Please."

He nodded. "Coming right up." He turned toward the bar, feeling eyes on his back. He was used to the stares, of course, but he hoped one particular person was staring at him, and maybe even checking out his ass.

Mason came back a few minutes later, drinks in hand. He frowned when the three women jumped away from each other, as if they'd been caught doing something wrong. Amelia's eyes dropped down to her feet while Kate and Sybil continued to stare at him, their eyes bulging.

"What, did I grow a second head or something?" he joked as he put the drinks down.

Kate's jaw dropped. "You're her—"

Sybil elbowed her friend in the side. "Thanks for the drinks, Mason," she said in a sweet voice as she reached for her wine. She leaned closer. "So, why don't you tell us all about *you*?"

Her sudden interest made him suspicious, and usually he walked away when people asked him about his past. But he couldn't leave, not when Amelia was standing there. Oh no, he wasn't leaving without her number. At least. "Not much to tell," he began. "I enlisted when I was eighteen. A year later after surviving the training, they started sending me out on missions." All three women were hanging on his every word, but all he really cared about was impressing Amelia. "I'm actually leading my own team soon. A special squad of shifters. First ever in the history of the SEALs."

"You're a polar bear, right?" Kate asked.

"Kate," Amelia warned. "It's not polite to ask."

"What?" Kate shrugged. "Polar bears are the largest bears in the world, you know. Well, except … never mind. But, it's obvious. Look at the size of him! And he's related to Tim."

"I'm sorry for my friend's rudeness," Amelia said.

"It's all right. I am what I am. So," he nodded at Kate's shot glass. "Why don't you knock that back and I'll get you a refill?"

"Really?" Kate drank the entire thing and clapped her hands together with glee. "How about another one? Or three?"

Mason laughed. "Coming right up."

When he returned with the said shots, Kate drank all three in succession, slamming the shot glasses down on the table as she finished each one. It wasn't that he wanted to get the wolf shifter smashed, but right now, he was desperate for a reason to stay with Amelia. He offered to buy Kate three more shots, and then eventually the whole bottle, then another. Kate was a shifter, so it took a helluva lot of liquor to get her wasted. About an hour later, she was finally rip-roaring drunk.

"Aaannnnd I kicked the guy out of my dorm room!" Kate slurred, her eyes glassed over. "He was a total douchebag!" She swung her head toward Mason. "You're not going to be a douche toward my friend, are you? You're going to treat her right? Since you are—"

"Kate!" Amelia's face went red.

"What? You're his *mmm!*—" Whatever she was about to say was muffled as Sybil clamped her hand over her mouth.

"Sorry about Kate," Sybil said. "I think I should take her home now."

Mason silently agreed as he took a sip of his beer. "Drive safe, then." Sybil hadn't had any more than the one glass of wine he got her, and being a shifter, she probably had burned off any alcohol in her system.

"Noooo! This was supposed to be my super special birthday night," Kate moaned. "I even got us the matching outfits!"

Amelia wagged a finger at her. "You need to learn to hold your alcohol."

"I'll burn it off in an hour or two," Kate said.

"And who knows what trouble you'll get into in that time?"

Sybil admonished. "I'll see you later, Amelia. Stay *safe*." Sybil's tone was teasing, with a hint of seriousness. "Let's go, you lush," she said to Kate.

"But it's only nine," Kate whined.

"Shut it. Party's over!" Sybil dragged her friend away, ignoring the she-wolf's protests.

Mason glanced at Amelia, who stared after her friends until they disappeared through the exit. Finally, he was alone with her. He wasn't going to be an asshole and try to coax Amelia away when she was celebrating with her friends, but he had hoped to get some alone time with her at some point. Maybe she wouldn't want to leave too soon. "Interesting friends you got there."

She laughed, the sound making him feel warm inside. "That's one way of putting it." Her baby blue eyes sparkled with mischief.

"How'd you all get together? A bear, a wolf, and a ... uh ..." He still didn't know what the heck Sybil was.

"A dragon."

"A dra—*what?*" He waited to see if she was kidding. When her expression didn't change, he realized she wasn't kidding. *Fucking A*. That tiny little thing was a dragon? "Are you serious?"

"As a heart attack." She flashed him a smile. "But don't you worry; she hasn't eaten any of my boyfriends. Yet." Amelia must have realized what that implied and went red.

Mason thought that was adorable. "Do you have one? A boyfriend, I mean." She shook her head, and the tightness in his chest loosened. "Good."

She blushed again. "Well, I should probably go—"

"Stay."

Mine.

Oh yes, she was going to be his all right.

The entire night, he'd felt drunk; not on alcohol, but on Amelia. Her honeysuckle and fur scent was intoxicating, and he could hardly keep his eyes off her. Once or twice, he touched her "accidentally"—his knuckles brushing against her hand when he handed her her beer, or his fingers grazing across the strip of bare skin on her back exposed by her top when he nudged her aside. It had sent the blood straight to his cock, and he knew there was no way he was going to leave tonight with just her number.

"I guess I could have one more drink," she said. "But why don't you let me buy you one? You've been buying all our drinks, in case you don't think I noticed."

"I'm glad you did," he said. He didn't care about the money though; he hardly had time to spend his pay since he was always on missions. But somehow, showing her he could spend money without a care was important, like he was telling her he could provide for her. "All right. It's a modern world, right? Women can pay too."

She smirked at him. "All right, you male feminist, let's go get that drink."

They walked over to the bar, and when he put a hand on the small of her back, she didn't protest, which he took as a good sign. Amelia signaled the bartender for two more beers, which the young man delivered quickly. She passed one glass to Mason.

"Thanks, beautiful," he said.

"You don't mean—"

"I do." He put the glass down without even taking a drink then leaned close to her. "I think you're the most beautiful woman in here. And the sexiest." Her breath hitched when he placed his palm on her lower back, feeling the warm skin there. "This outfit you're wearing"—he slipped his hand under the leather top—"made me think you were a bad girl when you walked in here."

"What makes you think I'm not?" There was a challenge in her eyes.

"I think you're sweet. And I bet you taste sweet too."

"Only one way to find out."

He stifled the growl, slipped his arm around her waist and pulled her close, molding her soft curves to him before leaning down to press his lips to hers. Jesus, she tasted as good as she looked. Warm, soft, and so willing. Her arms snaked up over his chest and around his neck, and she moved her head back so he could deepen the kiss. He slipped his tongue into her mouth, wanting more and more of her. When she pulled away, the loss of her lips made him groan.

Shit. He didn't normally lose his head this fast, but damn it, she was intoxicating. "I'm sorry."

"For kissing me?" she asked.

"I don't know what came over me. I shouldn't—"

"No!" She placed her hand on his chest. "I mean. I just thought," she looked around, a wary look on her face. "I want to be alone. With you. Do you have your own place? I don't live by myself."

Holy fucking moly. Mason thought he heard wrong, but the glitter of desire in her eyes told him he wasn't dreaming. Amelia wanted to go home with him. Wanted *him.* Maybe he wasn't the only one who felt that instant attraction and need. "I have a room at the Blackstone Motel."

"Will you … take me there?" she asked in a breathy voice.

He didn't answer her, but instead dragged her across the room and out the door. His ride was parked right by the door, thank fuck, as he wasn't sure he would make it another second without slamming her against something and having his way with her.

"This is you?" she asked, her eyes going wide.

Mason nodded and glanced back at his shiny new Harley. It was his prized possession now, the one luxury he owned. He'd never owned anything so expensive, but he figured it was a good reward for his promotion. He'd ridden it all the way here to show Tim. The old man was going to freak when he saw it. Tim loved Harleys and owned two custom models that he fixed up himself. During those months he stayed in Blackstone, his uncle taught him everything he knew about motorcycles.

"Jesus," she muttered, then looked him up and down. "You really are the whole bad boy package."

"Bad boy package?" he asked, glancing down at his outfit. He was just wearing his usual outfit out of uniform—leather jacket, white shirt, holey jeans, and riding boots.

"Yeah, that's what Kate called it," she huffed.

With a wicked smile, he grabbed her and pulled her to him, leaning down until he was just inches from her face. "If you want me to be a bad boy, I'll be a bad boy."

"I just want you."

He needed to kiss her again, and so he did. Slanting his lips against hers, he kissed her, full and deep, showing her how much he wanted her too. Hot damn, he couldn't get enough. It took all his strength to pull back, especially when all he wanted to do was bend her over his bike. "Still want to come home with me?"

She nodded. "Let's go."

Mason got on his bike, and waited for her to climb on behind him. He wasn't sure how they got to his motel room without crashing, especially with her arms around his waist and her luscious body pressed up against him. They barely made it up to his room, and as soon as the door crashed shut behind him, Mason slipped his arms around her and lifted her up. Amelia wrapped her long, lean legs around his waist. He could smell her arousal and feel the heat of her core despite the layers of clothing between them.

They landed on the bed and started ripping off each other's clothes. Off went her leather top and his shirt. As he unbuttoned his jeans, she shucked off hers and tossed them to the side.

Fuck, she was incredible, lying on the bed, her hair spread out and wearing only matching black underwear. He was so mesmerized by her he nearly forgot what he was doing until she glanced down at his hands. Remembering the task at hand, he finished off the rest of the buttons and shoved his pants and underwear down in one motion.

She sucked in a breath as her eyes landed on his thick cock, which was already fully hard at this point. He crawled over her, pushing her further up the bed.

"Mason," she whispered, reaching out to touch his face. Fingers brushed across his cheeks tenderly.

He closed his eyes then bent down, capturing her mouth in another kiss. This time, it was slow and sweet, his tongue tracing the fullness of her soft lips. At odds with his kiss, his hands moved urgently, as if trying to touch every inch of her all at once. He yanked down the cups of her bra, caressing her breasts. Her tits were just the right size and fullness in his hands, and the nipples were already tight with desire.

When he moved a hand down over her belly and down between her legs, she shivered and moaned into his mouth the moment his fingers grazed over her mound. He slipped his hand under the lace panties. *Jesus*. She was soaked.

Amelia thrust her hips up, and he obliged, slipping a finger into her. She was slick and hot, and he couldn't wait to get inside her. But first, he needed to see her fall apart.

He pulled his mouth away from hers and moved down between her legs. Ripping the panties off her, he pressed his mouth to her wet pussy lips. Fuck, she was even sweeter down here and her scent fully enveloped him until he couldn't smell anything but her honeysuckle scent, fur, and arousal. He teased her with his tongue, the tip lashing against the tightened bud of her clit. Amelia cried out his name, her fingers digging into his hair as he licked at her until she was shuddering with her first orgasm.

"You're fucking incredible." He looked up at her, her face flushed as she came down from her pleasure.

"I need you, Mason," she panted, reaching down toward him. "Please."

He would have been happy just eating her out the rest of the night, but his dick was so hard it was almost painful. With a grunt, he got up, grabbed his discarded jeans from the floor, and took out the condom from his wallet. He quickly rolled it on and positioned himself between her legs.

Amelia's arms wrapped around his neck, pulling him down for another searing kiss. Grabbing his cock with one hand, he pushed the tip right at her entrance, pushing and sliding inside of her slowly to allow her to adjust to him. She sighed against his mouth, a soft cry ripping from her lips as soon as he was fully inside her. God, she felt even better than he had imagined.

He slid his palms under her, lifting her hips as he began to move so he could get as deep as he possibly could. She cried out and mewled as he moved deep inside her, his pelvis hitting her clit at just the right angle.

"Mason, oh God! Fuck me harder."

And he obliged, thrusting into her savagely, loving the fact that she could take him and match him. Her fingernails raked down his back, the pain blurring with pleasure in his mind as his brain fried from the pure sensation. When she reached down between them to stroke her clit in time with his thrusts, he growled and fucked her even harder.

He could feel the tension building up in his body, and he urged her on, his fingers digging deeper into the soft flesh of her ass as he angled her body so she could take more of him inside her. When he felt her shudder and tighten around him, he didn't stop, despite the sweat building on his brow and the ache in his muscles. It didn't matter. Nothing mattered except Amelia and her pleasure.

Her orgasm was a beautiful thing, her skin growing flushed and her eyes closing shut as her body shook and her pussy squeezed around him. He gave her a few seconds before he let out a roar and slammed into her as he came. His arms went around her torso, holding her close as he rode out his orgasm. When he felt wrung out and the fatigue set into his body, he collapsed on top of her.

They lay there in silence for a few minutes, until Mason felt Amelia shift. He rolled away from her, his breathing heavy, and she cuddled up to his side. He found himself stroking her hair and pulling her closer. She laid her head on his chest, her soft cheek pressed to his damp skin.

Mason had never felt like this. Like he never, ever wanted to leave her. If he wasn't careful, he could easily fall for Amelia. But then again, maybe that wouldn't be such a bad thing.

CHAPTER ONE

Present day

Amelia Walker tossed the wadded up paper towel into the trash can and gave herself one last cursory glance in the mirror before turning away and walking out of the ladies room of The Den.

It was a Friday night, so the shifter bar was packed. Amelia was glad to see that despite the growth of Blackstone and all the other bars and restaurants she'd seen popping up around town, the people here still patronized The Den. It took a while before she finally felt comfortable enough to step foot inside, but she wasn't going to let *one bad thing* ruin a lifetime's worth of good memories of this place. Her parents had their twenty-fifth wedding anniversary here. Dad took her here for her first beer. Various friends had their birthday or engagement parties here. No way she was going to let that *one bad thing* dictate what she could do or where she could go.

Which was why she'd decided to come back to Blackstone.

Living in Messina Springs for the last four years had been good for her—not only for herself, but for her career. After graduating with her architectural degree, she needed to do a couple years of training anyway. The architectural firm, Moore & Jenkins, gave her more than enough hours of hands-on training on drafting, rendering, modeling, and other things she needed before applying to take the tests to get her license.

But, she knew she was needed here in Blackstone. Her family needed her. With everything that had happened in the last few months, Amelia wanted to be here, to protect her family and be right here with them if shit ever went down again. And nothing, not even *one bad thing*, would stop her.

"Do you think the proposal went well?" Amelia asked as she arrived back at their table.

Sybil Lennox was standing around the cocktail table with Dutchy Forrester. While Sybil was her oldest friend, Dutchy had only been in town for a few months. Warm and friendly, Dutchy had easily been accepted into the fold, and they all hung out regularly. Amelia thought she'd be more jealous of having a newcomer join their circle, but her friends never made her feel like she was being replaced.

Well, if she was jealous of Dutchy, it was because the petite redhead was just so cute and dainty, while Amelia felt like a clumsy giant compared to her. Her towering height had always made her feel insecure, especially throughout middle school when she was as tall, or taller than most boys her age.

"They're not back yet," Sybil answered with an eye roll. "So I can only imagine—" Her expression soured. "Never mind. I don't *want* to imagine."

"You know Kate will tell us in detail anyway," Dutchy said with a giggle.

Amelia grinned. "I'm glad for her." She could never

begrudge Kate any happiness, especially considering what had happened to the she-wolf in the past.

"Hopefully she'll mellow down," Sybil said. But, when she and Amelia looked at each other, they both burst out laughing.

"Hell will freeze over first," Amelia said, wiping the tears from the corner of her eyes.

"Or Petros will—" Sybil's expression changed, her mouth shutting and her lips forming a thin line.

"Sybil?" Amelia frowned and waved a hand in front of her friend's face. "Are you all right?"

Smoke began to curl out of Sybil's nose and a flash of gold scales rippled over her arms before disappearing back into skin. *Uh-oh.* Not a good sign. Dutchy gave Amelia a nervous glance. "Sybil? Are you okay?"

"Whatever you do, don't turn around." Sybil's teeth were gritted together and Amelia could feel her trying to control her dragon.

"Why not?" Of course now, she *had* to turn around. And then she figured out the reason for Sybil's outrage.

Despite the fact that he was hunched over the bar and she could only partially see his face, Amelia knew that figure anywhere. Mason Grimes. The *one bad thing*. Or rather, the cause of the *one bad thing*. Just her luck he would be here tonight, her first Friday back in town. She squared her shoulders. "So what?"

"So what?" Sybil asked, her voice half snarling. "What do you mean *so what*? That man—"

"Is nothing," Amelia completed. "He's nothing."

"He was your ex—"

"Boyfriend. If you could call him *that*." Amelia tossed her hair over her shoulder and crossed her arms over her chest.

"That's your ex?" Dutchy asked, her eyes widening.

"I know, right?" she laughed, making it lighthearted enough so it didn't sound too forced. Mason looked exactly the same as he did when she first met him—thick beard, gray beanie on his head, tattoos curling out from under his tight white shirt, jeans tucked into black riding boots. He was the very definition of a bad boy. "But, what can I say? We all make mistakes. And then we *move on*." She hoped her friends would get the message that she didn't want to talk about him. There was no way she was going to let goddamned Mason Grimes ruin her night.

"Guys! Guys!" Kate's boisterous voice made all three women turn their heads. "Petros asked me to marry him! And I said yes!" Her grin was as wide as the Brooklyn Bridge, but when her eyes landed on Sybil, her expression faltered. "Oh no." She then turned to Amelia. "You know."

"Know?"

Kate bit her lip, then glanced around. When she saw Mason by the bar, her shoulders sank. "I'm sorry, Amelia."

"Sorry?" Now she was confused. "Sorry about what?"

Kate looked at Petros, who then put his arm around her. "I … ran into Mason a while back."

So, Kate had seen Mason in town and didn't tell me. "You did?" Amelia controlled the tone of her voice so she sounded surprised, instead of angry.

"He saved her life," Petros added. "When Milos tried to kidnap her."

The she-wolf nodded. "I was in trouble and he came in and scared Milos off. And then … he told me he was moving here. Oh, and that he's divorced."

"Oh."

Kate threw her arms around Amelia. "I'm sorry! I should

have told you, but I was being selfish. I just wanted you back here and if you found out he was here too—"

"Kate, it's fine." She disentangled the other woman's arms, freeing herself from Kate's octopus-like grip. "It's not your fault."

"But he's—"

"I said, *it's fine*." The fact that Mason was also moving back to Blackstone hadn't fully sunk in yet, but she would deal with that later. "He's free to do whatever he wants."

"He's also free to jump off a bridge," Sybil muttered. "Do you want me to burn him? Or eat him?"

Amelia forced a chuckle. "Sybil, you've never burned, much less eaten anyone in your entire life. Don't waste your dragon fire and your appetite." She shrugged, just to emphasize she wasn't affected. "Blackstone is big enough for the both of us. Now," she turned to Petros, "tell us all about the proposal."

Petros nodded, and she was glad he was smart enough to understand that she wanted to change the subject. "As I told you, I was able to track down the seller of the car Kate wanted …"

Amelia pasted a smile on her face as she listened to Petros relay the story of how he planned the whole thing with buying the Chevelle Kate had been wanting, and then using it to propose to her in lieu of a ring.

The hairs on the back of her neck suddenly rose, and she knew that someone was looking at her. She didn't even bother to turn around, despite knowing who that someone was.

She spent the rest of the night laughing, drinking, and joking with her friends, enjoying the evening, and celebrating with the happy couple. Soon, Petros and Kate declared that they wanted to go home, and so they all decided to close their tabs and leave.

There was a slight chill in the air as they all piled out into The Den's parking lot. They waved goodbye to Petros and Kate as they walked off to the far end of the lot. Dutchy had parked her car on the other end and separated from Amelia and Sybil, who had ridden together in Sybil's Prius.

Amelia was tired. So very tired. She had become a good actress after all these years and convinced everyone she knew that she was okay. That her life was fine and everything was *great*. After a couple of hours of that charade, she felt the control starting to slip.

"Are you sure you're okay?" Sybil asked, stopping them before they got any further.

"I am, really, I'm fine." She put her hands on her friend's shoulders. "That whole thing happened a million years ago." Amelia looked Sybil straight in the eyes, just to show her she meant it.

"What are you feeling right now?" Sybil asked, concern marring her face.

"Nothing. Really, I'm so over it." She glanced back toward the doors. It was true. She felt nothing. She stopped feeling anything all those years ago when Mason broke her heart and their mating bond.

Four years ago...

"Mason ..."

"Hmmm?"

"Mason." Amelia said in an impatient voice. "Are you listening to me?"

He looked up at her, his lips and nose still nuzzling at the space between her breasts. "What is it, darlin'?"

She grabbed his head and pulled him up and away. "I said; why don't we go out tonight?"

"We already ate dinner." He gestured to the empty boxes of takeout on the small table beside the bed, then began to slide down lower between her legs. "And now I want my dessert." He flashed her a lascivious smile.

"Mason!" She laughed and swatted at him playfully. "C'mon, I'm trying to have a conversation here."

"I'm telling you I want to eat you out and you want to talk?" he asked, but his tone was lighthearted. He gave a faux exasperated sigh, and then propped himself up on his elbows. "Okay, darlin', spill."

"Well …" She twirled a lock of hair around her finger. "It's not that takeout and sex isn't great."

"It's fantastic," he teased.

"Ha! Yeah, but, you know … we've been going out for a week now. Not that I'm complaining about spending time with you, but … my friends are starting to wonder if I've fallen off the face of the earth. I was thinking we should go out."

"But we do go out."

"Ha." She smirked at him. *Going out* mostly meant ordering takeout or pizza, and then spending the night in his motel room. They hadn't even been to the diner or Rosie's, or anywhere else where there were other people around.

Still, Amelia couldn't believe how incredibly happy she was. And that she'd found her mate so early. Mason was perfect—everything she wanted in a mate. He was handsome, sexy, and brave, but he could also be sweet and kind. Plus, he was actually taller than her—both in human and bear form.

Her family had some sort of genetic trait that made their bears much bigger than normal grizzlies. Most shifters were only ten feet tall in their bear form, but her dad and brother were about fifteen feet. She was a female and smaller, but her bear was twelve feet tall on its hind legs. Being the largest bear in the world, Mason's polar bear was the same size as hers and twice as wide. They had shown each other their animals that first night together, when they went for a walk in the woods, and the fact that Mason didn't think anything of her monster size made her fall in love with him.

Was it too soon? No, they were mates. Dad said when he saw Mom, he instantly knew she was his mate. Her bear recognized Mason as her mate, as did his polar bear. It was strange however, that Mason never mentioned it. Or even said the word, mate. Had she read it wrong?

"Uh, Amelia?" Mason was waiting patiently, looking up at her from between her legs.

Oh yeah. "So, I was wondering, why don't we go to The Den? I'll call Kate and Sybil." She desperately wanted them to spend time with Mason, so they could see how awesome he was. They were happy that she had found her mate, but they kept hounding her because they wanted to get to know him too.

"Well, I don't know ..." There was hesitation in his eyes.

"I mean, the summer's almost over and I'll be headed back to school ..." Her throat closed up thinking about it. She was going back to finish her architecture degree at Colorado West U, and Mason's leave was almost over. He said it was unusual for SEALs to get this much time off, but since he was going to be leading a new team and could possibly be deployed for longer periods of time, his higher ups gave him time to settle any affairs and see family. In one week, he would have to report back to the naval base in San Diego, and he wasn't sure when he could next get time off. But surely they would work it out? They were mates and their animals wouldn't like being apart for long.

Mason's chest rumbled. "Yeah. I mean, I guess we could go."

"Great!" Sybil and Kate he already knew, and she'd told them right away about Mason being her mate, of course. Once he warmed up to the idea of hanging out with them, maybe she could start introducing him to their other friends, and eventually her family. Mom and Dad would be thrilled. "Let's go and get dressed—hey!"

Mason crawled on top of her and pinned her down. "But first ..."

They never made it out to The Den. They didn't even make it out of his room. As they lay in bed together, Amelia cuddled up to him. Her eyes were drooping as she pressed her cheek on his chest and whispered, "I love you, Mason."

She felt his chest rumble and he murmured something. As her eyes finally closed, she felt a warmth flow over her, like the softest blanket she'd ever felt. It settled on top of her, wrapping close around her and Mason. That night, she slept soundly, feeling such incredible peace and happiness in his arms.

CHAPTER TWO

Present day

"You sure you're okay, boy?" Tim's gaze bore straight into his soul.

"Yeah," Mason lied. "I'm fine. Do you want me to help with the chairs?" He glanced back at the main area of the bar. The staff had cleaned up all the empty glasses and bottles and swept up the floor. All that was left to do was to put the stools and chairs in order.

"You ain't on the payroll yet," Tim said. "Why don't you go home? I just asked you to come tonight to get you out for a bit and to stop you from moping alone in your apartment."

Mason shrugged. He didn't want a pity job from his uncle, but Tim assured him he needed an extra hand at the bar. The Den was short-staffed, with one waitress on maternity leave and the regular bartender filling in temporarily. He was going to start out the next day, but Tim told him to come tonight so

Mason could get comfortable in the bar and around the regulars.

"Nah, it's fine." Mason waved a hand at Tim as he walked over to one of the tables. "I'll get this all done and then I'll be on my way."

Mason began to lift the chairs and put them up on the tables, glad to be doing something with his hands rather than sit and do nothing. The entire night, the only thing he *could* do was sit and think, and it was driving him up the wall.

The last year of his life had been hell, and moving to Blackstone was his last chance to make it right. Tim had given him the solution to his problems. He was hesitant, given the circumstances around the last time he left, but Tim reassured him that Amelia Walker wasn't living there anymore. Of course, her family was here, and he knew there was a chance he'd run into her, but he was so desperate.

Mason knew he was going to run into her eventually, he just didn't think it would be so soon or his reaction would be this bad.

Years after, it still hurt his goddamn heart to see her again, even from a distance. Seeing her laugh and chat with her friends like she was totally unaffected made him want to destroy everything in sight. His animal was in a tear, ripping him up from the inside. *Yeah, I know it's all my fault,* he told his bear. Not that it would do any good. The damn thing had only become more wild and fucked-up in the head over the last couple of years, especially with the shit he'd seen and the things he'd gone through and done.

Amelia hadn't changed a bit. She was still the most goddamn beautiful woman he'd ever known in his entire life. Still sexy and confident with an air of sweetness about her. He couldn't resist her back then, and he still couldn't resist her now. He watched her like a hawk the whole night, and if she had known he was there, didn't show it and completely ignored him. Why wouldn't she? He had been a complete bastard to her.

Mason slammed a chair particularly hard, jolting his thoughts back to the task at hand. No, he couldn't live in the past. There was no way he could change it, nor make it hurt less. Besides, he had other things to worry about.

When he was done with the entire floor area, he glanced up at the clock. It was nearly four in the morning. He should go home and get some sleep before his important appointment the next day.

While he may have fucked-up his life with one bad decision after another, it was going to stop now. He was going to turn things around, starting tomorrow. That meant he couldn't afford any missteps and he certainly couldn't be distracted, not even by Amelia Walker.

Four years ago …

"What are you doing?" Mason asked, looking over Amelia's shoulder.

"Huh?" Amelia whipped her head around, nearly smashing her face against his. "Oh!" She reeled back, then quickly grabbed something on the table, hiding it in her hands.

"What's that?"

"Nothing," she said, her face going red.

"That didn't seem like nothing," he teased as he nudged her

over so he could slide into the booth beside her. "C'mon, show it to me."

"Nuh-uh."

Mason could see that she was trying to hide a smile. "It's just you and me here, darlin'." He looked around at the empty diner. He finally did take her out, but not to The Den or anywhere in Blackstone. Convincing her it was more romantic for them to ride over to Verona Mills, he took her to dinner at one of the fancy hipster fake diners in the newer part of town. He still liked the old school ones like the one in Blackstone, but he wasn't comfortable there.

It wasn't that he was ashamed of being with Amelia. But rather, it was the opposite. He didn't want *her* to be seen with him. A couple of days after that first night, he had confessed to Tim that he was seeing her. He was surprised and explained who she was. To say Mason was shocked was an understatement. Her father was one of the most respected men in town, and her uncle was one of the wealthiest dragon shifters *in the world*. He was surprised because nothing about Amelia screamed rich, spoiled princess. She didn't wear fancy clothes, never asked him to take her to expensive restaurants, nor did she have a superior air around her.

Still, he should have known he was punching way above his weight. That first night when he saw her, he didn't really know who she was; all that he cared about was getting in her panties. And she was the one who invited herself to his place. It had been the most intense night of his life. And after that first time, they took a walk in the woods. She had shown him her bear, and just as he thought, it was magnificent. He'd never seen anything like her—powerful and large and overwhelming. His bear was smitten, and he too was head over heels.

"Please?" he asked again. "Were you doodling or something?"

"Well, it's not really anything yet." She put hands back on top of the table and opened her palm, spreading out a crumpled piece of napkin. There was a drawing done in red ink, her fingers stained with the same crimson color.

"What is it?" He leaned down and peered at the napkin. It looked like a house or a cabin.

"Well, it's a dream project of mine. I mean, it came to me in a dream, kind of." She laughed and tucked a lock of hair behind her ear. "My dad and my brother live in the woods, in cabins they designed and built themselves. My dad loves building as a hobby and my mom does interiors. Anyway, they told me that they'd build one for me too, someday, if I ever wanted my own place. But I've always wanted to design my own house, so that's why I got into architecture and design."

"Tell me about this house," he said.

"It's going to be two stories, with an attic. This is the main living room and it's going to have a sunken …"

He listened to her, soaking in every detail of her dream house. Mason wasn't sure what it was about her, but whenever she was around him, it was like nothing or no one else existed. And when she was like this—talking about something she was truly passionate about, she was even more magnificent.

He was in love with her, he was sure of that. Just the other night, he had whispered it to her. He said it to her, over and over again while she slept, because he was too goddamned scared to tell her while she was awake. Because he knew he wasn't worthy of her.

But something had changed a few nights ago. He didn't know what it was, but he felt closer to her, like his very soul was linked to hers. It was like he could sense her moods or guess what she was going to say before she said it. He brushed it off, thinking it was just his imagination.

"Well, what do you think?" she asked when she finished describing the house.

"Beautiful." He leaned down and kissed her. "The house is great too."

"Mason!" she swatted him on the shoulder and laughed.

He was going to tell her, he decided right then and there. He'd take her out and tell her that he loved her and wanted to be with her. They could work it out and he would take every leave he could to be with her, and maybe start planning to retire. He glanced down at the napkin on the table, and then back into her beautiful sky-blue eyes. Yes, that sounded like a great plan.

CHAPTER THREE

Present day

"And this is your workspace," Erin Matthews said as she led Amelia to the large drafting desk in the east corner of the open-plan office. "It's not a private office, but—"

"Oh no, this is great." Amelia placed her hand on the brand-new drafting desk. The space was well-lit and roomy, plus the window looked out into the trees of the forest around the area. A shiny new computer with a large screen sat on top of a stylish table. "My old office used to face an alley behind a Chinese restaurant," she said with a chuckle.

"I'm really happy you decided to take the job as my designer," Erin said.

"*I'm* happy you decided to open your firm here." Amelia counted herself lucky she got this opportunity so quickly. Although she already had the number of required hours to start the licensure exams, she didn't want to just spend all her time studying, which is what she would have done if she wanted to move back home since there was nowhere in Blackstone she could do her training. At least, not until Erin opened her firm, Erin Matthews Architecture and Interiors, or EMAI for short.

"I know Blackstone isn't as glamorous as Denver or Messina Springs, but I could feel this place was special. My husband and our kids are tiger shifters, which is why we wanted to move here right away from Chicago," Erin explained. "I'm starting from scratch, but I already have some clients lined up which is why I needed the help."

"I'm glad to be here, really," she assured Erin. "Working at Moore & Jenkins was a dream come true and I got the training I needed. But I just wasn't growing there." And that was true. At a big architectural firm, she was really nothing more than a cog in a wheel. Working under Erin meant she would be able to do more than just draft and render. Plus, Amelia already had interior design skills learnt from her mother, so she would be doing those for their clients as well.

"Awesome." Erin clapped her hands together. "I'm going to go and get some coffee from the cafe across the street. Do you want anything?"

"Why don't you let me get it?" Amelia offered. "Please. Let me kiss up to the boss. It's my first day, after all."

Erin laughed. "All right, I won't say no to free coffee. Just black, please."

"No prob." Amelia gave Erin a two-fingered salute, and then headed out the door.

The office was located on the top floor in one of the commercial buildings in South Blackstone, a new development in town. The buildings were only half filled for now, but according to Matthew Lennox, CEO of Lennox Corp., they expected to be at 90 percent occupancy by end of the year.

EMAI's office building was located on Twelfth Street and First Avenue, and they shared the floor with two other businesses—a law firm and a marketing company.

Amelia pressed the call button for the elevator. She watched as the numbers on the digital display began to rise, then the loud *ding* indicated that the car had arrived. As the doors opened, she stepped forward, but didn't expect anyone to be on the other side.

"Sorry!" she said as she bumped into someone. The hairs on her arms rose, as she scented something she recognized—fur, with the clean, crisp scent of fresh mountain air. A pair of hands steadied her as she staggered back and she found herself staring up into the light blue eyes of Mason Grimes.

"Amelia," he said in that achingly familiar rough voice of his.

For a brief moment, Amelia felt a spark of life in her. And then she felt something else she hadn't in a long time—desire.

While all the emotion she ever felt for Mason may have disappeared, she was still a woman, and—dammit—he was still as sexy as ever. He wasn't in his usual white T-shirt today. Mason was actually wearing a long-sleeved shirt with a collar, though his muscled shoulders and arms strained against the fabric. He was wearing a nice pair of jeans and his boots, but his beard was shorter and neatly trimmed, and his blond hair was slicked back. Ugh, it was unfair how he could look so good in absolutely anything.

"Hello, Mason," she managed to say.

"What are you doing here?" he asked, his brows drawing together in confusion.

"Me? I work here." She nodded toward EAMI's door. "And you?"

"I have an appointment." He didn't elaborate. Of course he

didn't. Getting anything out of Mason had always been like pulling teeth, and she didn't expect him to be any different after four years.

The growing silence was getting awkward, so she decided to break it. "Well, I guess I'll see you around." She sidestepped him, and though her feet were like lead, she managed to walk into the elevator. When she turned around, Mason still stood there, staring after her. The door began to close and relief started to creep in. Unfortunately, Mason was too quick and he managed to squeeze his hand in between the doors, preventing them from closing.

"Was there something you wanted?" she asked.

"Yeah, uh …" He glanced to the left, toward the door to the law firm, and then back at her. "I … I have to go, but I just wanted to say"—he took a deep breath—"for what it's worth, I'm sorry."

She shrugged. "I know." Maybe he didn't remember that night at all. That's why he didn't recall how he told her sorry over and over again four years ago, when he left her crying in the rain. "Was there anything else?"

His jaw hardened. "No, there's nothing else."

He released his grip and as soon as the doors shut, Amelia braced herself with one hand as her knees turned to jelly. *Breathe. You can do this.*

She pressed the button for the ground floor and as the elevator car began to descend, the tightness in her chest eased and she regained control of her legs. Still, despite all that, her first run-in with Mason had gone better than she thought it would.

Forget about him, she told herself. *It's over.*

But she couldn't help the curiosity pricking at her. What was Mason doing there? Was he looking for a job? All Kate had said was that he was moving to Blackstone and was divorced. Did he leave the SEALs? And what about his—

The *ding* indicating that she had arrived on the ground floor interrupted her thoughts just in time. No, she wouldn't think about … *that*. The *one bad thing*. The reason she left Blackstone; her secret shame. That was ancient history and she didn't really give a damn what Mason was up to now. She finally had her life together, back at home with her family and friends, and she wasn't going to let him ruin things for her again, not when she worked damn hard to forget him and what he did to her.

Four years ago ...

Amelia tried not to fidget as she sat by herself at a table in the dining room of Giorgio's Italian Restaurant. She glanced at her watch for what seemed like the hundredth time. She thought maybe time was passing too quickly, but no. Mason was over an hour late now. The waiter had stopped checking in on her and instead, left her alone with the glass of red wine she'd been nursing since she sat down.

Was Mason always late? She didn't know. They usually met at his motel room and by the time she knocked on the door, he was there, waiting for her. It was like they couldn't get enough of each other and the moment they were alone they were ripping each other's clothes off.

But something had changed a few days ago. She couldn't quite pinpoint when, but deep in her heart she knew what it was. The mating bond.

She had heard her parents and Uncle Hank and Aunt Riva talk about it, but it seemed like such an intimate thing that neither couple offered details. All they told their children was "you'll know it when it happens." It was different for each couple, apparently. She huffed unhappily. *It would have been nice to know for sure right now.*

Surely, it must have happened. The bond had formed. She couldn't describe it, but it was like she felt what he felt and knew his moods. Each time she was away from him was agony and when they were together, she'd never felt more content.

Her bear was different as well. Happier around him. Though neither one of them said it aloud, he must have felt it too. In fact, he was the one who asked her out tonight, telling her he had something important to tell her.

Excitement had filled her. Mason was leaving in two days and he was going to tell her something important and wanted to have dinner at the most romantic restaurant in town. She hadn't heard him say 'I love you' yet, nor did he call her mate. The latter actually made her more annoyed; she had always thought it was cute when Dad called Mom "mate" playfully, though she could see the love in his eyes. Until she'd met Mason, she hadn't known how much she'd longed for someone to call her mate.

The crack of thunder jerked her out of her reverie. It had started to pour the moment she got in and she thought that might have caused Mason's delay. It wasn't fun to ride in the rain, but surely he would have tried to call her if he couldn't ride or was going to be late.

The soft beep from her phone on the table indicated that her battery was about to die. *Ugh, should have replaced that thing long ago.* But, practical person that she was, she decided to hold off on buying a new one until after graduation. She brought an external battery but had left it in her car.

She signaled the waiter to come over and explained that she was just going to grab her battery, but would leave her phone here. When the waiter nodded, she stood up and headed toward the door.

The wind howled as she exited the restaurant. She was getting ready to make a run for her car when she felt the familiar feeling wash over her.

"Amelia."

She turned to her left. Mason was standing just outside the awning, the rain pelting him. Immediately, she launched herself at him. He was soaking wet, and she would be too, but she didn't care. She was just so glad to see him.

"Mason, I've been so worried!" She rubbed her nose on his wet shirt, trying to scent him despite the rain. "Where have you been?" He remained silent, and finally she noticed how stiff his body was. And that he didn't return her hug. "Mason?"

He gently pried her away from him. "Amelia, I'm sorry."

"It's okay, you're here now," she said, looking up at him, searching his face. His expression was stony and his eyes were hard, like glacial ice. "So you're a little late. It happens to everyone and—"

"That's not it." He turned away from her, and then cursed, his hands curling into fists at his side. A raw burst of power from his bear emanated from him. Anger. Rage.

Amelia staggered back. She had never seen him like this, nor had she ever felt his animal so ... agitated. He said that there was something wrong with his polar bear, but didn't elaborate on it. She could guess his childhood had been rough and that sometimes caused problems between shifters and their animal side. But she was never afraid of Mason's polar bear. In fact, her own animal adored his, ever since that first night.

"Tell me what's wrong," she whispered. "Please."

Mason looked up at the sky and cursed again, then slowly turned to her. His expression was inscrutable. "I have to go."

"Go? But you're not supposed to report back to base for another two days."

"No. I mean, it's something else." He took a deep breath. "I don't know how to say this, so I'll come right out and tell you. A couple months ago … there was this girl."

Amelia reined in her jealousy. "What do you mean 'girl'?"

"I swear to you, it was way before we met. My team and I were back on a 3-day break after a tough mission … we went to this bar just off base and there was this girl … I was drunk and so was she, and I went home with her."

Bile began to rise in her throat, but Amelia pushed it down. "So what? Like you said, that was months ago. I wasn't a virgin or anything when we met."

"It's not—" He shook his head. "I left right away. Didn't leave my number or anything, but she managed to track me down through my CO. Called me an hour ago, right before I came here." He let out a strangled cry. "She … she said she's pregnant."

Amelia was pretty sure she heard the word pregnant and understood what he was saying, but the ringing in her ears made everything in her brain go haywire. A knot began to form in her chest, and her bear roared with anger. It clawed at her, wanting to get at Mason. She leashed it back, and she felt a strange tug in her gut. "I don't understand … what are you going to do?"

"My CO's furious at me. He'd been there that night.

Everyone saw us and ... turns out she's an admiral's niece." He ran his hands down his face. "Fuck, I don't want this. I can't ... this is fucking insane."

She felt the numbness creeping in slowly, from the tips of her toes, inching up her legs, over her body until she felt like she was encased in ice. Hot tears began to flow down her cheeks. "I don't understand. Why ... how could it be?"

Surely they could work it out. Something similar had happened to her mom and dad. Ben wasn't her mom's biological kid, and he had arrived in their lives while her parents were still dating. Of course, Ben's mom had passed away, which is why he ended up in Blackstone.

"I need to go and fix this." The words were like a door slamming in her face.

This wasn't fair. She had finally found her mate, and now ... "Mason, please!" She threw herself at him. "Please! Maybe ... there's been a mix-up. I mean, you could figure it out and I can wait—"

"I'm sorry, Amelia." He might have been crying too, but she couldn't tell because of the rain. "This wasn't how it was supposed to be. I was taking you out tonight because I wanted to ask you to be my girlfriend and try to make this long-distance thing work."

But I am yours, she pleaded silently. *And you're mine.* "Things shouldn't be like this. We can't—" A sob broke from her throat.

He shook his head. "Please, don't make this any harder. This is a kid we're talking about. *My* kid. And no kid of mine is going to grow up the way I did."

There was a steely determination in his eyes, and despite the hurt she was feeling now, Amelia knew he was right. She wanted to rage—at life, at fate, at Mason—but she couldn't.

This was a human being they were talking about, and he helped bring this person into the world.

He took a deep breath. "I'm heading out now. Back to base. Sort things out with my CO. Maybe they'll let me keep my team."

Ah yes, there was that, too. Mason loved being a SEAL and she knew it would crush him if he was discharged. "Go then."

"Amelia—"

"Just go." She didn't recognize her own voice. "Now." *Before I throw myself at you and beg you to not leave me.*

Mason gave her one last glance, but she refused to look him in the eye. Instead, she looked straight ahead, letting the rain blind her. He began to walk away. Away from her, until he disappeared from her blurred vision.

Amelia wasn't sure how long she stood in the rain. Someone had come out of the restaurant and asked her if she was okay, but she didn't answer.

She thought her life falling apart and her heart being torn to pieces would have been more loud or violent. That there would be more screaming or raging. But no. There was only silence.

CHAPTER FOUR

Present day

Mason couldn't move. He couldn't breathe. He couldn't think. He stared at the cold metal doors, unable to do anything else.

Mine!

The words roared in his head. He hadn't heard it in years.

He thought seeing Amelia from afar had been difficult. Being near her had been worse. They said that the opposite of love wasn't hate, it was indifference, and he understood that saying now. Having her act like nothing was wrong when his insides were churning and his bear was tearing him up was devastating.

The day he left, he could hardly look her in the eye. Her face had haunted his dreams for the last four years. Leaving her that day was the worst mistake of his life. At least, now he knew that. But hindsight was always fucking twenty-twenty. He didn't even want to think what his life would have been like if he'd stayed and told his CO, Admiral Peters, and *that bitch* to go pound sand.

It was all done. Frankly, he should have been relieved. And today, Amelia was fine and he couldn't begrudge her that. And like Amelia, Mason told himself he should move on too.

His bear disagreed. Loudly. Like it was telling him that Amelia was *not* fine. But he shut it up. *There are other more important things*, he reminded it.

With every ounce of his will, he forced himself to turn away and walked toward the law office of James D. Moynahan. His appointment was for 10:00 a.m., and he was already running late.

"Good morning," the receptionist greeted as he entered through the glass door. "Mr. Grimes?"

"Yeah," he said with a nod. "Sorry, I'm late. I ... was delayed outside." *Because of Amelia.* His mind was still on her now. Normally he trusted his bear's instinct. And it was telling him something was wrong with her. Why should he ignore it now?

"Let me check in with Mr. Moynahan. Please have a seat."

Mason sat down on the plush leather couch in the waiting room. As the receptionist picked up her phone, he found himself zoning out again, his mind going to Amelia. There was something there that was just ... not right. She looked the same, but his instinct told him she wasn't the same. Hell, she didn't even *smell* the same.

"Mr. Grimes? He's ready for you." The receptionist pointed to the door on the left.

He put it out of his head for the time being. All those years, dealing with Jenna at home and his dangerous missions, he had learned to compartmentalize well. Right now, there really were more pressing matters that needed his full attention.

"Thanks," he said, and walked toward where she directed him and opened the door.

James D. Moynahan was sitting at his desk, staring at his computer. But as soon as he walked through the door, the attorney turned his head. "You must be Mr. Grimes. Nice to meet you." He reached over to offer his hand.

"Same here." He gripped the other man's hand. Shifter, of course.

According to Tim, Moynahan was a fox shifter and one of the best attorneys in town. "Those foxes are smart and wily," Tim had said. "But Moynahan's honest and won't do you wrong."

He gestured to a chair in front of the desk. "Please sit down and we can begin."

Mason took his seat, shifting uncomfortably in the small, delicate modern chair. He didn't have a suit, and Tim said he didn't need one, but he'd got dressed in his nicest shirt anyway. "Thanks for agreeing to see me."

"Of course. Tim's a good man," Moynahan said. "Got me out of trouble at The Den one night. I literally owe him my life. Now, what can I do for you?"

His hands gripped the chair and when the wood creaked under his fingers, he let go. Tim said he could trust Moynahan, and the attorney had agreed to cut his initial consult fee to a small percentage, which had been a relief since he really didn't have the cash to spare right now. But, he wasn't sure he was ready to share the most intimate details of his life with a stranger.

Sensing his hesitation, Moynahan leaned forward and put his hands on the desk. "Mason, as your attorney, I have a duty to not only do what's best for you, but to keep everything you tell me confidential. I won't tell anyone, not even my mother. Now, please do tell me what I can do for you."

Mason hesitated for a moment. "It's my ex-wife. Jenna. We've been divorced for a year."

"And the divorce has been granted?"

He nodded. "What I'm here for is my daughter. Cassie. She's three." Mason took his phone out of his pocket and opened it to the lock screen. There was a picture of a young toddler, with dark-as-midnight hair and pretty brown eyes. She was smiling and looking into the camera. Mason couldn't count how many hours he'd spent the last couple of weeks just looking at her picture, missing her so much his chest hurt. "I need to get her away from her mother."

"Is she being abused?" Moynahan asked. "If so, we can get an emergency removal."

"Not physically. At least I don't think so." He took a deep breath. "I don't know where to begin."

"I really need to know more about your situation in order to give you the best advice possible." Moynahan leaned back into his chair. "Why don't you start from the beginning?"

"All right." *Here goes nothing.* "I met Jenna four years ago. It was a one-night stand, but she got pregnant. She's also the niece of one of the admirals back at the base in San Diego." Mason clasped his fingers together. "We got married. At the time, I felt like I had no choice. This was a kid we were talking about. Plus, my CO basically told me to do the right thing or else." He swallowed down the bitterness, or else it might have consumed him. "She had the kid and—" He stopped so suddenly that his teeth clacked together.

"And then what?"

"And then ... I went on with my enlistment. The navy had

me going on these missions. I was gone a lot, but I spent every minute I could with my Cassie."

"And Jenna?"

"We fought all the time. Finally, it came to a point that she would just leave and go to her parents' house whenever I was home. At least, that's where *she said* she was going. In truth, she'd been cheating on me the whole time, with several guys." It was fucking embarrassing, but he really didn't give a shit at that point. The marriage had been a sham from the beginning. "I didn't care. I loved spending time with my daughter."

"When did things come to a head?"

"About a year and a half ago. I was sent to a black site in South America. No communication for weeks. And when I did come back, I found out she'd had me served with divorce papers." That bitch found out exactly when he would be gone and decided to time it so he wouldn't find out until after he came back. "The judge gave temporary orders while I was away, including full custody of Cassie to her. Finally, I came back and the divorce went through, but she retained full custody. Legal and physical."

"But you got visitation rights?"

"I did, but she fought with me every step of the way. She only does the bare minimum and threatens to take Cassie away from me whenever I try to fight her. She also drained all of our savings, transferring everything from our joint account to her own account. I also still have to pay her alimony, but I can't file charges against her or try to adjust the payments, or she'll make sure I won't have any visitation rights. All my visits are already supervised." God, he really wanted to wring Jenna's neck right now. "She told the judge I was violent. Basically alluded that I was dangerous without lying outright. Because of what I am."

"What about the navy? Didn't they help you at all?"

"I resigned my commission when things got hairy with Jenna." He gritted his teeth. "She was the niece of an admiral. I didn't have a choice." Things really went to shit then. It wasn't pretty. "My lawyer basically rolled over and let them do whatever they wanted." His chest tightened, remembering his desperation. He'd been screwed over for a *second* time in his life, and to think he'd risked his hide going on those dangerous missions. Life really wasn't fair.

Moynahan cleared this throat. "Now, you said your wife abused your daughter? Do you have any documentation to prove it?"

"That's the thing." That desperation began to sink into him again. "It's not that Jenna hurts her, it's just that she ignores Cassie. Gives the bare minimum of attention, but once she's done, she'll pawn her off on her parents or friends and go out and party with her boyfriend, Doug." Mason hated that douchebag. "Or worse, stay at home and get drunk around Cassie."

"How do you know this?"

"Well..." He wasn't proud of this but he had to lay it out. "I snuck onto the base and watched the house. She was playing on the carpet in the living room and there were bottles of alcohol everywhere. Doug and Jenna were in the bedroom the whole time." He knew it was wrong and against the law, but he had been so desperate to see Cassie. That's why he couldn't go to the police and report her.

Moynahan frowned. "I'll pretend I didn't hear that. But, did you try to call child services anonymously?"

He nodded. "At least twice. But by the time they get onto the base, Jenna and Doug clean up their act and look like the perfect parents. I think someone in the navy police tip them off when CPS is on the way."

Moynahan placed his elbows on the table and clasped his hands together. The lawyer was quiet for a few moments before he spoke. "I have to be honest with you, Mason, I'm not familiar with how things work on navy bases. I'll need some time to do research. Maybe I can call a couple of people and see what we can do to prove neglect or abuse, then see about an emergency removal."

"That would be great."

"But, I assume you'd want to get full custody?"

"Yes."

"Considering what your ex-wife may have said in court and based on the fact that the judge only granted you supervised visits, that may not be so easy."

Mason sighed. "I know." He had already consulted with a lawyer back in San Diego and he knew what Moynahan was going to say. Mason had no real job and no money, plus combined with what Jenna said during the custody hearings, it didn't look good. CPS will always do what's best for the child and that could be placing Cassie in foster care. "That's why I'm here. I want to become a resident of Blackstone."

Moynahan's face lit up. "Ah, of course. The Lennox Foundation."

"It was Tim's idea." The Lennox dragons were the founders of Blackstone. They declared the town under their protection, and The Lennox Foundation provided education and healthcare for all its citizens, especially shifters who were seeking sanctuary from a world that hated them. Tim had suggested he come to Blackstone, find a job and a house, and then he'd be able to show a judge that he was more than capable of taking care of Cassie. Of course, there might be *one* problem with that plan, but he'd worry about that later.

"It's a good start," Moynahan said. "How's the job search?"

"Tim's giving me a couple of hours a week at The Den." That wasn't nearly enough, but he had to start somewhere.

"Have you thought of working at the mines?"

"Uh, I'm not sure that would be a good fit." That had been Tim's first suggestion, but Mason immediately nixed it when his uncle told him who the foreman was.

"Well, you can't be too choosy. But, how about your own place?"

"I have an apartment now," Mason said. "But it's a studio that Tim helped me get. I'm working on getting a bigger place."

"All right then, it looks like you're doing the best you can." Moynahan stood up. "I'll call someone I know at CPS now and see what I can find out. I can always help you file a change of custody agreement."

Mason got up as well. "Thank you. Anything you could do would be great." Moynahan seemed like a legit guy. He knew this wouldn't be cheap, but he would do anything to get Cassie back. Taking care of the legal fees was his next stop after this. It wasn't going to be easy, but it would be worth it.

"I'll call you when I have something." Moynahan's eyes narrowed at Mason. "Are you sure there's nothing else you need to tell me?"

It was almost eerie the way his gaze seemed to pierce through him. His eyes flashed gold for just a second. He had heard rumors about some shifters who could tell if you were lying, but he never believed them.

Mason swallowed hard. "No. Nothing at all."

For some reason, telling James Moynahan the story of how his entire life turned to shit made Mason feel better. *That talking about your problems and feelings bullshit works after all.* Or maybe it might have been because for the first time in eighteen months, he finally felt a small spark of hope.

His next errand though ... this was going to hurt. Big time. But he had no other choice.

Mason got on his Harley, revved the engine, and backed out of his parking spot. He memorized the directions from his phone and fifteen minutes later, found himself outside J.D.'s Garage, just a few blocks off Main Street.

Mason already had an idea of how much James Moynahan's legal services were going to cost. Even at a discount, he knew he wouldn't be able to afford them. Since he was forced to give up his command before he hit the twenty year mark in the navy, he wasn't getting full retirement pay, and what little he did get went to Jenna. His ex-wife worked under the table as a waitress so the alimony amount was significant. If he knew that all that money was going to Cassie, he wouldn't have balked, but he was pretty sure Jenna and Doug used most of it to live it up while neglecting his daughter.

And so, he had no choice but to give up one of his prized possessions. Tim had suggested J.D., who owned a car garage in town. J.D. had a lot of contacts and would be able to help him find a buyer who would take the Harley at a fair price.

Mason drove into the compound, and then parked outside the small office on the right. He walked up to the door, but found it locked. Peering inside, he didn't see anyone, so he walked off toward what was the main garage workshops—three medium-size warehouse-type buildings along the north and west side of the compound. There were several people walking around and working on cars.

"Hey man," he said to one of the burly mechanics wearing a uniform coverall that said "J.D.'s Garage" on the chest, "I'm looking for J.D."

The man looked around, then nodded his head toward the left. There were two people chatting by a white Mercedes raised up on a platform. Mason gave the man a nod of thanks.

The smaller of the two men had his back to Mason, so he caught the eye of the larger man. He was about Mason's height and size, with a thick, black scraggly beard, and short hair buzzed close to his scalp. He had a serious look on his face as he spoke to the smaller man, but his eyes flickered to Mason's as he approached.

"J.D.?" Mason asked.

"Yes?"

But it wasn't the large man who answered. It was the smaller man who turned around to face him. And, much to his confusion, it *wasn't* a man. The figure was dressed in loose coveralls, but the face that looked up at Mason was small and delicate, with porcelain-like skin and hazel eyes framed by long lashes. Despite the streak of grease down her cheek and the messy blonde ponytail tucked under a trucker hat, Mason would have been blind not to notice that J.D. was a *woman*.

"Uh..."

J.D. crossed her arms over her chest and raised a brow at him. "What do you want?" She was obviously used to people being taken aback by her sex.

"I'm Mason Grimes."

The mechanic's face changed, her expression lighting up in recognition. "Oh! Tim's nephew!" She rubbed her hands down her coveralls and thrust her palm at him. "Nice to meet you."

Mason shook it. The scent of motor oil and grease hid whatever her animal's scent was, but she was definitely a shifter. He'd forgotten what it was like to be around others like him. He and his team were a close-knit group, but they were the only other shifters he had hung out with regularly.

"So," she said as she took her hand back. "Give me a second here, then I'll be right with you, okay?" She turned back to the gigantic man. "All right Bruno, if that fussy bitch who owns the Mercedes even raises her voice or looks at you wrong, you come to me, okay?"

Bruno nodded silently.

"You were only doing your job. If she has a problem, then she better take it up with me. Now go help Junior with the Toyota and make sure he doesn't use the wrong hose again." She shook her head, then looked at Mason. "Okay, show me your bike."

He led her over to where he'd parked his Harley and as soon as J.D. saw it, she let out a long whistle. "Jesus H. Christ. That's one sexy ride. If I had a dick, I'd be sporting a big chubby right now."

Mason bit his lip to keep from smiling. She wasn't at all what he'd expected.

J.D. moved in for a closer look, leaning down to inspect the engine. "She's a beaut." She shook her head. "You really want to sell her?"

"I have to."

"I'd take her, but I don't ride. I can see she's a damn fine piece. Where'd you have her customized?"

"Nowhere," he said. "I mean, I did, at home."

Hazel eyes bulged in surprise. "You did all this?"

"Yeah. Took a couple of years, since I only had time here and there." When things got too heated with Jenna, which was nearly all the time, he would hide out in the garage and work on his Harley. After Cassie, it was the one thing he looked forward to when he came home. It was a good thing he had the presence of mind to keep it stored at a friend's house whenever he wasn't home, since who knows what Jenna would have done if she had gotten her claws into his bike.

"Where'd you learn to do this shit?"

"Tim taught me everything he knew. I lived with him for a couple of months while he was working on his own Softail." Mason wanted to get a job while he stayed with Tim, but he had been too young to work at The Den or at the mines. And so, to pass time, Tim had taught him how to tinker around with motorcycles and even let him help with the Softail's rebuild. "And everything else I didn't know, I just looked up on the Internet or asked other mechanics for advice."

"You didn't have any training?"

"Nope. But everything seemed easy enough to learn on my own."

"No shit?" She slapped a hand on her thigh. "I respect that. I learned everything from my pop and when he died, I took over." She nodded at the painted sign over the office. "His initials were J.D. too, so I didn't even need to change the sign," she said with a laugh.

"Must've been convenient for you."

"Yeah, well, Pop was hoping for a boy, but he got me," she said wryly. "So, about the bike ... I can make a couple of calls. Off the top of my head, I know at least one guy who might be interested. Do you have an idea of what you want for it?"

Mason rattled off an amount.

"Hmm, I really don't know much about bikes, but I can run that number by a friend of mine, and then we'll see if we can get some bites. It might take a couple weeks to find you a fair price."

"That's fine." If Moynahan wanted money right away, he'd find a way to scrounge it up. His next stop after this was to drive over to the gas station. He'd seen a hiring sign on the door the other day when he came in to pay.

J.D. scratched her chin. "Good. Send me a couple of pics today and I'll put out some feelers. I got your number, so I'll let you know when I find a buyer."

"That sounds great." The heavy weight pressing down on his shoulders lightened by about a couple of pounds. But his problems weren't over, not by a long shot. "I should get going. I promised Tim to come over and help him out around the house."

"No prob. See ya around, Mason." With a wave, J.D. turned on her heel and walked back to the work area.

Mason threw a leg over his Harley and started the engine. He wanted to go home and sleep. Or maybe head to Tim's and tell him the good news. But, something made him drive all the way back to South Blackstone, back to the building where he'd run into Amelia. He parked across the street, just off to the side so anyone coming out wouldn't immediately notice him.

At twelve noon, people began to file out of the building for their lunch break. His eyes scanned the crowds, and soon enough, Amelia came walking out with a middle-aged woman, chatting amiably as they left.

Mine!

Yeah, yeah. Stupid bear. *Why don't you stop being an ass and tell me what you think is wrong with her?*

His keen eyes scanned her, looking her over. She was still damn beautiful and sexy, even in her plain suit jacket, skirt, and heels. But he was looking for something else. Something he may have missed when they ran into each other. But what the hell was it?

His bear growled and scratched at his insides, urging him to go to her and make sure she was okay. It was going stir-crazy now as she got further away from him.

No way. He was not going to chase after Amelia Walker. He'd ruined her life once, he wasn't going to do it again.

CHAPTER FIVE

"You know, there are other bars in town we could go to," Sybil said as she pulled into the parking lot at The Den.

"Like Argo's?" Amelia teased.

Sybil winced. "You guys are never going to let me live that down, are you?"

Amelia chortled. "I wasn't the one who set a girl's hair on fire."

"I was doing it for Kate," the she-dragon grumbled as she maneuvered into a spot. "Anyway, like I said, we don't have to come here. Even Kate said we could just hang out at her loft."

"I said we're going to The Den, and I mean it. I need to celebrate my first week back here." Amelia let out a snort. She knew her friends absolutely loved her, but they were just getting too much. They had been walking on eggshells around her all week, she could feel it. Like they were careful about what they said and were ready in case she had some sort of breakdown.

Well, of course they were. When Mason left and her life fell apart, Sybil and Kate were there for her. She didn't go home to her parents' cabin, staying with Sybil instead. She wouldn't eat, sleep, or get out of bed. Her friends had to force her to go out into the world. At one point, she was contemplating leaving school. Oh, she could still remember the fight she had with Sybil, and the she-dragon threatened to fly her back to school herself. She did go back eventually, but her grades suffered and Kate begged, berated, and beat her into getting them back up.

Yes, she understood why her friends were acting like this; after all, they were the ones who saw her lowest lows and helped her pick up the pieces. And to think, they didn't even know the *worst* of it.

Amelia hardened her resolve. It was all behind her now. Her run-in with Mason proved that she could act like a normal person around him. Besides, she wasn't going to let him dictate where she could go around town. Blackstone was *her* town. It was where she grew up and where she would stay for the foreseeable future. If he had a problem with her, *he* could leave. "Now," she said to Sybil. "Come on, let's go."

Sybil followed behind her as she walked to the front door, her head held high and shoulders straight. As she walked in, she saw a couple of people she knew, and stopped to say hi to them. Finally, she went to their usual table, where Kate, Dutchy, and Christina Lennox, Sybil's sister-in-law, were waiting.

"I told you, we don't have to come here," Kate said, her face drawn into a deep scowl. Her eyes darted over to the bar and Amelia froze for a second when she followed Kate's gate. Sure enough, Mason was there, slinging drinks and taking orders.

"And I told you, it's fine," Amelia snapped. Kate and Sybil exchanged looks. *The look*. And for a moment she just wanted to knock their heads together. "You know how fine I am about this? Let me show you." She made a beeline toward the bar.

As she drew closer, her heart skipped a beat. Dammit, why did he have to be so attractive? His muscles rippled underneath his tight shirt, and it looked like he added more ink on his arms. Memories flooded back in her brain, of running her hands down his chest, over his perfect set of six-pack abs and lower still. Her core clenched, thinking of all the times they'd been together. Maybe if she hadn't thrown herself into her work for the last four years, she wouldn't have had the longest dry spell in her life. But then again, despite their broken bond, Amelia couldn't bring herself to sleep with anyone else, not even to get Mason out of her system.

She walked confidently toward the bar, stopping until she stood right in front of him. He had his back to her and was reaching over to the top shelf to grab a beer glass. When he turned around, their gazes clashed, and Mason went stone still.

"Can I have a beer, please?" she said. Somehow, she relished the shocked expression on his face.

"Right away," he said, tearing his gaze away. He put the glass in the tap and filled it, then slid the glass over to her. "On the house," he said as she reached for her wallet.

She considered ignoring him and slamming the cash on the bar anyway. Or maybe even throwing the beer in his face. But she was here to prove Sybil and Kate wrong. "Thanks." She pivoted on her heel and walked back to their table. When she got there, she gave Kate and Sybil a smug smile.

"I guess you really are over him," Sybil said.

"Guess so." She took a sip of the beer, the alcohol calming her nerves and her shaky knees. She was ready to move on from this conversation. "So," she turned to Kate. "What was the urgent reason why we absolutely had to meet tonight?"

"This is my pre-bachelorette party," Kate declared.

"What's a pre-bachelorette party?" Dutchy asked.

"Well, it's when we all come together to plan my real bachelorette party!" Kate said.

"We couldn't have done that over dinner at home?" Christina said. "Or via group chat?"

"No!" Kate stopped a passing waitress. "Can I get five shots of tequila please?" When Christina groaned, she added, "actually, why don't you go ahead and bring me the whole bottle." She flashed Christina an evil smile.

"Why do we need tequila?" Sybil asked.

"It's an important part of the pre-bachelorette process," Kate said smugly.

Sybil rolled her eyes. "Oh, so this is all an excuse to get drunk?"

"Excuse me, I don't need an excuse to get drunk." Kate thanked the waitress when she returned with the shot glasses and the bottle of tequila. "Now, let's get down to business!"

"You're just sad because Petros had to fly to Lykos and you're all alone," Christina pointed out.

"I miss him." Kate sighed and pulled out her phone.

Amelia expected her to stare lovingly at a photo of Petros or something, but instead, she put the phone under her shirt. "What the heck are you doing?"

"I'm taking a photo of my tits," she said matter-of-factly. The flash went off, and she pulled the phone out, then tapped on a few buttons. "And now I'm sending it off to Petros."

Sybil spit out her wine. "Why the hell would you do that?"

"Because Petros loves my tits," she explained. "He says that each time he thinks of me, I'll know it because I'll think of him too. And then I said when that happens, I'm going to send him a photo of my boobies."

"Do we dare ask how many photos he has now?" Dutchy said, a delicate brow raised.

"Well there was the three that I sent him last night while his plane was taking off—"

"I think that was a rhetorical question," Sybil said dryly.

Amelia couldn't help but smile as she took a sip of her beer and listened to her friends banter. Oh, how she missed this. Four years of being away had been good for her, to help her ease the ache of the memories, but it had also been lonely. But she couldn't risk exposing her secret shame, finding out about the *one bad thing*. Eventually, someone—maybe her Dad or Ben or Sybil or Kate—would have noticed it.

"Are you okay?" Sybil leaned over and whispered.

"I'm fine." Amelia's damn traitorous body and unconscious mind made her turn her head back to the bar. Her hand tightened around her glass as her gaze zeroed in on Mason.

He wasn't alone, which wasn't unusual given that he was working behind the bar. But a woman—cute and blonde—was leaning over the top, smiling up at him as he placed a glass with amber liquid in front of her. She reached over and handed him a napkin, which he took and crumpled into his palm. He was leaning down to whisper in her ear, and the sight made Amelia's vision blur and pressure build behind her eyes that she quickly turned away. She made a grab for her purse.

"… And I want all penis party favors!" Kate exclaimed. "Dick straws, dick banners, dick balloons, dick cupcakes, dick headbands. The works!"

Sybil groaned. "I am not wearing a dick headband, Ka— Amelia? Where are you going?"

Amelia made an exasperated face. "Kate reminded me—I have this absolute *dick* of a client who wanted to see fabric samples as soon as our supplier sent me the pics." She took out her phone. "Let me take care of this asshole and I'll be right back girls! Save me some tequila."

She quickly turned around and made her way to the exit. Someone, call the Academy because she deserved an Oscar.

The cool mountain breeze made the evenings a little chilly this time of year, and Amelia breathed in the fresh air as she pushed the door open and stepped out. She missed this. Missed looking up at the stars. Missed smelling the scent of pine everywhere. Leaving was the only way she could have survived the broken bond, but it still meant being away from the only home she ever knew.

Taking a last, deep breath, she pulled up her metaphorical big girl panties and psyched herself up to go back inside and continue ignoring Mason. But as she turned, she heard the door swing open.

"Yes, Ma'am," Mason said into the phone tucked against his ear, his eyebrows drawn into a deep frown. "I'll be there as soon as I can." He was slipping the phone into his jacket pocket but stopped when his cool blue eyes landed on her. "Amelia?"

"Mason," she nodded, then sidestepped around him. She was barely halfway to the door when she felt a warm, calloused palm on her arm.

"Is there something the matter? Are you okay?"

A spark of anger lit up in her chest. "Please don't touch me."

"Amelia, please," he said. "Tell me what's wrong."

Her head whipped around. "What's wrong?"

"We should talk."

"I have nothing to say to you," she said, her voice surprisingly even. "I think I've made that perfectly clear." She wrenched her arm away from him.

"Please," he begged again. "I can't stand this ... you're just ..." He glanced down at the phone in his hand and let out a deep breath. "You're different," he began. "The other day, when I ran into you—"

"Shut up. Just shut up!" The anger and resentment came out of nowhere. Or maybe it had been bubbling up and was now boiling over. The broken bond. Leaving her home and her family. Everything that she *lost*. And she was damn tired of pretending that it was okay. "You have no right to speak to me! Or touch me! How dare you pretend to care now!"

"I always cared about you," he said.

The words made her heart clench, which only made her angrier. "Stop lying, Mason."

"I'm not—"

"Then why did you leave?"

Mason gritted his teeth. "What the hell was I supposed to do, Amelia? Abandon my kid?"

That was the problem. No matter how much she hated that he left, she couldn't get mad at the circumstances. Still, the rage she felt blinded her. "You were supposed to be with me! My bear said you were ours. Our mate. You broke the bond. And now I'm ..." She didn't want to say it. Oh God, she couldn't say it. She'd been in denial all this time.

"Amelia ... you and I are mates?"

Was he insane? Or stupid? Did he hit his head on a mission or something? "*Were* mates," she said bitterly. "Why do you keep denying it? You must have felt it too. We bonded, that night when we were supposed to go out with Sybil and Kate, but we stayed in instead."

"I honestly ..." He scrubbed a hand down his face. "I didn't realize that's what it was. Amelia!" He tried to grab her but she evaded his grasp. "I had no idea. Please, believe me. My dad, he died when I was eight. My mom was human. Tim was the first shifter I met until I came to Blackstone."

Amelia stood there, staring at him. His words were slowly sinking in for her. But, did she believe him?

"I didn't know. Anything. And after, I'd heard about mates from the shifters on my team, but I never paid attention. My bear must have known, but—"

A ringing from his pocket interrupted them and Mason took his phone out and looked at the screen. "Fuck!" He gripped the phone tight in his hands. "Amelia, I have to go right *now*."

"I'm not trying to stop you." *Not anymore.*

His face drew into an anguished expression. "I don't want to, but I really need ..."

"Just leave," she said. *That's all you ever do.*

"This isn't over, Amelia."

"It's been over for a long time." She didn't wait for him to say anything else, instead headed back into the bar. She pushed against the storm door and walked into the small entryway, where she could be alone.

She leaned against the wall and took a deep breath. Mason really was a jerk. After he left, she had hoped that maybe he had changed his mind. Or that it was all a mistake. But no, he didn't call or even text her to say what happened. He just never came back. The coward.

She was left to pick up the pieces, and then keep the biggest secret of her life. The *one bad thing*. Somehow, because of the broken bond, her bear had *disappeared*. Gone from her body, just like that.

She was hurt and in denial all those weeks, but she confirmed it one night. She tried to shift into her bear, but she couldn't. It just wasn't there anymore. She cried hard that night, maybe even harder than she did for Mason, at the loss of her constant companion for twenty-one years.

And so, she left Blackstone. Learned to pretend everything was okay. She hardly came home the first two years, in fear of having her friends and family discover her secret. She learned to cover it up over the years and put on an act. But in truth, she felt hollow without her bear.

This was all Mason's fault. Whether he was lying to her or telling her the truth about not knowing about mates, it was his fault that her bear was gone. She hardened her resolve to keep away from him. He had broken her once, and she would be a fool to let him do it again.

CHAPTER SIX

Mason had just tossed the napkin the perky blonde had handed him into the trash when he got the call.

"Hello?"

"Is this Mr. Mason Grimes?" The voice on the other end of the line was stern and business-like.

"Yeah. What do you want?"

"Mr. Grimes, my name is Marsha Hill, I'm with Child Protective Services in San Diego. I have some bad news."

Mason wished he was tired. If he had been a normal human being, the bumpy, red-eye flight from Colorado to California would have wiped him out. But no, he wasn't tired at all. He was all riled up, and so was his polar bear. The energy around him was enough to make even the humans on the flight wary of him. His seat mate had unbuckled his belt and switched to a different row as soon as the fasten seatbelts sign had turned off.

The entire flight, his mind was reeling. Ping-ponging back and forth from thoughts of Cassie to Amelia. Worried about

Cassie. Processing his conversation with Amelia. Wanting to kill Jenna. Wanting to hold Amelia in his arms and beg for forgiveness for hurting her.

It had been a shock, but he should have known. He had never really forgotten about Amelia all these years. When he finally started hanging around other shifters, mostly the guys on his team, he began to learn more about their kind. They'd been joking around, getting drunk after a mission, when someone brought up the subject of mates. Not wanting to sound stupid, he went along with the conversation, pretending he knew what they were talking about. He was squad leader after all. Even though the conversation was over his head, something must have stuck in his brain. Amelia was *his mate*. That's what his bear had been trying to tell him. He was a fucking moron for ignoring it.

It was almost 5:00 a.m. when the plane landed and the sun was peeking over the horizon. He gripped the wheel of his rented car as he pulled into the driveway of the Child Protective Services headquarters. He wasted no time parking in the first available slot and headed into the building. He gave his name to the receptionist, who then picked up the phone.

"Mr. Grimes?"

Mason turned around at the sound of the familiar voice. Marsha Hill was a middle-aged African-American lady wearing horn-rimmed glasses. Her suit was rumpled, but professional-looking. Not that he was criticizing her, as he probably looked like shit himself. "Where is she? Where's Cassie?"

"She's fine." Hill's voice was even and calming. "She was a little dehydrated and hungry when we found her, but the doctor said she's okay. Come with me and I'll show you to her."

Hill had led him down the hall on the left. When she stopped in front of one of the doors, he didn't wait and threw it open.

As soon as his eyes landed on Cassie, he released the breath he'd been holding since he got the call. "Cassie."

"Daddy!" A small bundle leapt into his arms. His daughter was safe and sound. That was all that mattered. He squeezed her tight as her small body racked with sobs.

"It's okay, baby," he said. "I'm here. Daddy's here."

"I … was … scared," she said in between hiccups. "I … didn't … know anyone."

Mason could only imagine what it was like for Cassie, being surrounded by strangers. He was going to kill Jenna and Doug. He would hunt them down and give them both slow, painful deaths. But, he had to stay calm, especially here. "Baby, everything's going to be okay." He kissed the top of her head and rubbed his palm up and down her back. Rocking back and forth, he began to hum the song he used to sing to her. After a few minutes, Cassie's body began to feel heavy and her breathing evened. He was satisfied, at least for now, and so was his bear. But it remained edgy, pacing inside him, waiting.

Glancing around him, he saw a cot in the corner and gently laid her down. He didn't want to let go of her, but she was safe and there was no way in hell he was leaving here without her. But first, he had to take care of some business. He pulled the soft pink blanket around her, then stood up.

Hill had remained in the room the entire time, waiting patiently for them. Mason walked to her and spoke in a quiet voice. "I know it was a rush to try and get back here ASAP and we didn't have time to talk. But, can you run me through what happened in detail?"

Hill nodded. "Let's go somewhere we can talk privately."

Reluctantly, Mason followed Hill outside but he didn't move away from the door. He planted himself outside and crossed his arms over his chest, signaling that he was not taking another step.

Taking her glasses off, she began to explain. "Yesterday, one of your neighbors, Amy Travers, was coming home from work when she noticed Cassie wandering by herself on the lawn. She immediately went to her and asked where her mom was, and all Cassie said was that she woke up alone that morning. Ms. Travers called 911 and the police department called us."

Mason's jaw clenched thinking of how Cassie must have felt, waking to an empty house. His polar bear seethed and he was only barely able to leash it in. "Did you find Jenna?"

"Mr. Grimes, the police have a warrant of arrest for your ex-wife and her boyfriend, Mr. Doug Brown, for armed robbery. They hit several convenience stores over the past couple of days."

"What. The. Fuck!" He clenched his fist. He knew Jenna and Doug were terrible people, but robbing convenience stores? "Have they caught them yet? What are the police doing? Why would they rob convenience stores?"

"I'm afraid you'll have to ask the police those questions, Mr. Grimes." Hill put her glasses back on.

Mason's mouth pulled into a hard line. "What's going to happen now? When can I take Cassie home?"

"Well, normally in this case as the parent we would release her to you, but I read in the files that you don't have legal or physical custody."

"The custody agreement is all bullshit and I had no choice," he said, a snarl at his throat. "I don't care what it takes, you can't keep her away—"

"Mr. Grimes." Hill's voice was even, but firm. "I'm trying to help you here, so kindly don't raise your voice at me."

Mason's shoulders sagged. "Please, Ms. Hill. I'll do anything to keep her."

"I understand. Now," Hill looked around. "I noticed that CPS had made two previous visits to your home inside the base, but they found nothing out of the ordinary. But the fact that they had to make the visits concerned me. I suggest you file for emergency custody. Given the circumstances, a reasonable judge would grant it in a couple of hours."

"I'll do it now." He could take Cassie home, maybe today.

"But—"

"But what? Jenna's gone. She just abandoned Cassie. Who knows what could have happened to her while—"

"Mr. Grimes," she warned.

"Sorry." Goddammit. "Go on."

"There is one more thing." Hill looked around her and lowered her voice. "When I came across your custody agreement, it was mentioned that you were a shifter. Is that correct?"

His stomach soured, knowing where this was going. "Yes."

"When I saw this, I thought we might need special assistance. I called in one of our other caseworkers. A wolf shifter. And she told me something odd." Hill looked him straight in the eye when she said the next words. "Mr. Grimes, Cassie is fully human."

"Yes."

"But you're a shifter."

"Yes."

"I'm not stupid, Mr. Grimes." Hill's expression was grave. "I know what that means."

"Oh yeah?" Mason felt his animal's hackles raise. "My

name's on the birth certificate. Jenna insisted on it." The bitch threatened to have him dishonorably discharged if he didn't sign it. But he had the last laugh now. "She's my daughter."

"But not biological—"

"She's *my* daughter." *No ifs and buts.* His bear agreed. "If Jenna wants her back, then she'll have to come out of whatever hole she's hiding in and take her away from my cold dead body. Now, tell me what I need to do to get my daughter home."

Mason was finally exhausted. Dealing with CPS, the cops, and the courts would have turned anyone into a zombie, even a shifter. But, thirty-six hours later, he and Cassie were on the first flight back to Colorado.

She was fast asleep. She had thrown a fit when she woke up again and Mason wasn't there, refusing to calm down until he came back from giving his statement to the cops. He had to pacify her by running back and forth from CPS to the courtroom.

But it was all over, for now at least. The police were still hunting down Jenna and Doug, but no one could find them. They had left the house in the middle of the night, and no one had seen or heard from them. They could be anywhere by now, and the police suspected they may have made a run for the border.

His polar bear was out for blood, urging him to find Jenna and Doug and kill them. Cassie could have gotten hurt or worse. No one hurt their cub and would get away with it. *Soon,* he said. *But for now, we take care of Cassie.*

When Mason came out of the airport, a small suitcase in

one hand and Cassie in the other, Tim was already waiting for them just outside Arrivals. Since he didn't have a car seat or even a car, he had no choice but to ask for help.

"Thanks for coming."

Tim nodded, then his eyes landed on Cassie. The little girl's jaw dropped and her eyes widened. If Tim noticed that Cassie wasn't a polar bear like them, he didn't show it. "Hello, Cassie," he said. "I'm your great-uncle Tim."

Cassie let out a squeak and buried her face in Mason's shoulder. "It's okay, baby." He nuzzled at her temple. "Tim's here to take us home." But Cassie refused to look at Tim. "Sorry. It's been a long flight."

"Don't worry about it," Tim said. "She'll need some time to rest and adjust. Let's go. I got things ready for you two."

Much to his surprise, there was a car seat waiting in the back of Tim's truck. His uncle explained that he had stopped by the fire station. They had several of them in the firehouse as one of the services they offered was to teach new parents how to install seats. The chief had said he could keep it for as long as he needed it.

The drive back to town was silent. Cassie was still exhausted and only fussed a bit when Mason put her in the seat. Soon, they were pulling up to his place.

The studio apartment was right on top of a hardware store and located across the road from The Den. It belonged to one of Tim's friends, and he helped him rent it out to vacationers in the summer and whoever else needed it the rest of the year. Tim offered it to Mason for a huge discount, saying the owner owed him one. Mason didn't have the luxury of keeping his pride, though he would work on finding a better place once he got a better-paying job.

"Thanks," he said to Tim. He carried Cassie into the apartment while Tim brought in the small carry-on. Mason hadn't had much time to pack up Cassie's stuff, but he got the essentials. Much to his dismay, Cassie didn't have a whole lot of clothes that fit her anyway, and they would have to go shopping. The good news was at least, the judge ordered the alimony payments stopped since Jenna was now a fugitive and Mason would be getting his retirement pay in full this month.

He placed Cassie down on the futon and pulled a blanket over her. After kissing her on the forehead, he stood up and faced Tim.

"Here." Tim's held out the keys to Mason.

"What?"

"You can't bring her around on your bike," he said. "You take my truck until you get it all settled."

"I can't—"

"Shut up and take it, boy," Tim ordered.

Mason sighed. "You should at least keep my Harley then." He fished in his pocket and handed the keys over. "Keep her safe until I find a buyer."

"Right. Now"—he turned to the door—"let's talk outside."

Mason nodded and followed his uncle outside. As soon as the door closed, he turned to him. "I know what you're going to say. Cassie—"

"Is safe here with you," Tim interrupted. "But, are you going to get to keep her?"

"Kind of." He filled him in on what had happened. "I was on the phone with Moynahan the whole time. He says he's going to file the paperwork so I can get full custody. No way in hell Jenna's getting near Cassie, even if she somehow wormed her way out of trouble." With the charges of armed robbery, running from the law, and child abandonment, Jenna had basically dug her own grave.

"So, it's done then? She's yours?"

"Basically. But everything has to be done by the book. I'm getting the works—welfare checks, home visits, interviews—you name it." He was cautiously hopeful, having been fucked over too many times. "The lady at CPS says she'll try to delay sending the paperwork over to the welfare services office here in Blackstone so I can get the place ready before the first home visit. I'll get her a bed, clothes, toys, whatever she needs. Then start looking at a bigger place."

Tim's face went stormy. "You do know who works at the social welfare office here in Blackstone, right?"

"No."

"Sybil Lennox. It's a small office, and knowing you're a shifter, they'll probably send her."

Fuck.

"Sybil's a good kid," Tim assured him. "By the book. She won't take anything personally. But you should probably sort everything out as soon as you can."

Mason liked his hide un-burnt, so he decided to go out and go to the store as soon as Cassie woke up. But, speaking of Sybil Lennox … "Wait, Tim. Before you go, there's something I need to ask you." The question had been in the back of his mind the entire time. Now that he had Cassie, he could finally focus.

"What is it?"

"It's about … mates. Do shifters really have mates?"

"Some don't, but others do. No one really knows for sure how it works. You don't know anything about mates?"

This was embarrassing, but he had thought it over. Tim was the only other shifter he knew in town who could get him the answers he needed. "No."

"No one talked to you about it? Not even your dad when he was alive?"

Mason shook his head. "After the funeral, you know my mom took me to Tennessee. There were no other shifters in town. And then you know how she was …" He gritted his teeth but didn't continue. That was all ancient history, and he was over it. He wasn't the first kid to get beat-up by his parents. Things came to a head when he was seventeen and he shifted and nearly killed his step-dad. His mother had been furious and called the cops on him, and that was when he decided to run away to Blackstone.

"That mother of yours is a piece of work. You know it was because of her your dad stopped speaking to me." Tim rubbed his jaw with his meaty hand. "I always thought she hated the fact that your dad was a shifter, but he was the only guy in a uniform who managed to get her pregnant."

Mason grimaced, knowing that was probably true. His mother had been a base bunny, looking to get knocked up by a serviceman and live the good life of a navy wife. The irony wasn't lost on him. "So, what can you tell me about mates? I'd only ever heard about them from my team."

"Shifters are private about stuff like that, which is why you don't exactly find stuff like this in books or the Internet. Besides, who'd want scientists poking their noses into their business and studying them like animals?" Tim huffed. "I don't know much, just from what I've seen and heard myself. When your animal finds the one you're fated for, it tells you."

Mason felt the blood drain from his face. That's what his bear had been telling him. Amelia was his fated mate. "And … what about the mating bond?"

"Apparently, it just happens, not right away of course.

You'll accept her as your mate and she'll accept you and you form the bond. It brings you closer together and ..." He frowned. "I don't really know the rest of it." He raised a brow at Mason. "Anything you need to tell me? Why are you asking me?"

A soft cry from inside the apartment made them both turn their heads. "Sorry. I'll explain later."

"Go take care of your daughter," Tim urged. "Call me if you need anything. And take the time you need."

"Thanks, Tim." With one last wave, he turned and hurried into the apartment. Cassie was sitting up in bed, looking around her. Mason quickly went to her side. "It's okay, baby. Daddy's here. I'll be right here. I won't ever leave you." Cassie blinked sleepily and nodded, then laid back down and closed her eyes.

Mason took a deep breath. Cassie was here. Finally. He hated the circumstances, and his blood still boiled thinking of Jenna and Doug, but their loss was his gain. As he watched over Cassie, Tim's words rang in his brain.

So apparently, he and Amelia had bonded while they were together for those twelve nights. Each of those nights were still crystal clear in his mind, and he could probably pinpoint when it changed. He thought Amelia had been sleeping and he was so tired himself. He told her he loved her and it happened.

She said the bond was broken. How could she tell? Were there signs? He'd been caught up in the whole situation with Jenna that he didn't even notice. Fuck, he really was a bastard.

Somehow, he knew he had to make it up to her. Amelia would never take him back, especially not with the baggage he carried. He imagined that Cassie would forever be the reminder of what he'd done to her and there was no way he was giving up Cassie for anyone. Still, his sense of honor told him that he had to make things right with Amelia, no matter what it took.

Cassie stirred, jarring him out of his thoughts. *But first things first.*

CHAPTER SEVEN

AMELIA WALKED down the aisle of the curtains section, stopping to take a look at the display of sheer fabric. She already had the decorative curtains picked out, but she just needed the sheers for privacy. After finding the right type and length, she got the package from the shelf, and then placed it inside her half-full shopping cart.

Checking the paper in her hand, she saw that next on the list was throw pillows. *Thank God for big box stores.* She would be able to furnish and decorate the house she was renting. She'd thought of moving into one of those fancy new apartments in South Blackstone, but the thought of being in a box didn't appeal to her. No, she had wanted something with space and a garden. Just her luck, she saw an ad in the Blackstone Community website about a house for rent that fit the bill—it was a spacious three-bedroom at the edge of town with a small front lawn and a spacious backyard. Now, she only had to fill the inside to make it a real home.

It's not that she didn't want to support the local stores in Blackstone, but she just loved the convenience of having everything in one place. This particular brand was well-known for having stylish and affordable pieces, and since they didn't have one in Blackstone, Amelia drove all the way to the Verona Mills Commons strip mall so she could do her shopping. Her place was looking bare as she didn't have time to shop with the move and the new job. Finally, it was Sunday and she decided it was time to get things together.

Should I get plain or printed? Amelia looked at the designs on the pillows. *Maybe I should take a picture and send it to Mom.* Laura and James Walker were still on their round-the-world retirement trip, but her parents always made time for her and Ben if they wanted to talk. Since she got back to Blackstone, she'd found herself missing them so much more and taking them up on their offer when she could. Just this week, she'd video-chatted with them twice.

As she was deciding between the stripes and the houndstooth print, a loud, ear-splitting scream pierced the air. Amelia frowned. This was the one downside of shopping at a big-box store. With a deep sigh, she put the striped pillows in her cart. She still needed bed sheets, so she pushed the cart to the next aisle. As she turned the corner, the wails became louder and she saw two figures in the middle of the aisle. The smaller one, a little girl, was obviously throwing a fit, while the larger figure was bent down, trying to calm her down.

Amelia rolled her eyes and stopped, ready to back out of the aisle and call it a day, when the larger figure stood up and turned to face her. Light blue eyes grew wide with surprise. *Well, this was awkward.*

"Amelia?" Mason asked. He didn't move, and instead continued to stare at her.

Amelia forced herself to look at the little girl next to him. She wasn't stupid; she knew who it was. Sometimes, when she simply couldn't help herself, she'd imagine what Mason's kid would look like, the one he had abandoned her for.

The little girl was probably no more than three or four, with long dark curls down her shoulders. She was wearing a pink dress, sandals, and leggings that were a tad too short for her. Her face was all red and blotchy, with snot coming out of her nose and tear streaks down her smooth, chubby cheeks.

Amelia always thought that if she ever found herself face-to-face with Mason's family, she wouldn't be able to stand it. That she would cowardly walk away, or run and hide. Instead, something inside her made her want to go over and see what was wrong with the little girl. As if on instinct, she left her cart behind and walked over, kneeling beside the girl.

"Hello," she said. "What's your name?"

The girl looked up at Mason, and then at her. "Cassie."

"Cassie," she repeated. "What a pretty name." She reached over to tuck a stray lock of hair from the girl's cheek. Then, Amelia froze. Her eyes searched Cassie's face.

While her own bear was no more, Amelia still retained the enhanced strength, healing, and more importantly, senses of a shifter. And her senses were telling her one thing: Cassie was definitely a human. She smelled like a human and felt like a human. *I don't understand.* Who was this girl with Mason?

"Cassie," Mason said, clearing his throat. "Say hello to Amelia."

"Daddy, who is she?" Cassie asked, her face drawing into a look of suspicion.

Well, that made her even more confused, but she composed herself. "I'm your daddy's … friend." She took a handkerchief from her purse. "Can I help you get cleaned up?" Cassie hesitated, but then nodded. Amelia gave her a reassuring smile and wiped the tears and snot from her face.

"There, don't you look pretty! Now, what's the matter, sweetheart?"

"I want to go home," she said, her bottom lip trembling. "I just want to go home. To my *own* bed and my toys and Mommy."

Amelia tried to ignore the pang in her heart at the words. *Where was the girl's mother? What the heck was going on?*

Mason knelt beside them, placing an arm on Cassie's small shoulder. "I'm sorry, baby. I told you, Mommy's gone. She's ... taking care of her aunt in New York. You'll be staying with me from now on."

Tears began to form in Cassie's eyes. "But I want to go home!" Her mouth twisted as she broke into a sob.

Mason rubbed the bridge of his nose with his thumb and forefinger. "Let's just pick some sheets and go, okay? You need it for your new bed."

Amelia didn't know why, but her heart ached, seeing more tears pour down the girl's cheeks. "Wow, a new bed? That sounds like fun. And new sheets! Are you going to pick a princess one?"

The girl stopped sobbing, and then turned to Amelia. "Eww, no." Cassie grimaced. "I hate princess things. And I hate pink." She looked down at her dress. "Daddy packed only my pink clothes."

She gave a little laugh. "You know, I hated pink too when I was growing up."

"You did?"

"Uh-huh," Amelia said with a nod. "My mom would always buy me pink everything. And I was kind of a tomboy. I loved going camping with my dad and my brother. Fishing, swimming, stuff like that. But Mom would always tell me to act like a lady and put me in dresses." She laughed.

"Does your mom still make you wear pink?"

"What? Nah. When she realized I wasn't going to ever like pink and princess stuff, she helped me redecorate my bedroom into something I liked."

"She did?"

"Yup. She let me pick out my own bed, my bedsheets, and my furniture." Amelia smiled fondly at the memory, and she missed her mother even more.

"Could you help me?" Soft brown eyes looked up at her. "Please, 'Melia?"

"Cassie," Mason began. "I don't think—"

"Sure." The words were out of her mouth before she realized it. She cleared her throat and stood up. Cassie immediately grabbed her hand, and Amelia couldn't ignore the way her gut clenched. "Now, what's your favorite color?" She clutched Cassie's palm into hers.

Cassie thought for a moment, then shouted. "Green!"

Amelia laughed. "Mine too. Maybe we could start with some sheets." She looked back at Mason, who was staring at her, his mouth open. She realized she must have overstepped her bounds. "I'm sorry," she said, letting go of Cassie's hand. "I probably should go—"

"No!" Mason said quickly. "Please. I—we could use your help."

She gave him a weak smile and nodded. "Okay, well, why don't we get those sheets?"

Amelia didn't notice the time, except that it seemed to go by quickly. She helped Cassie pick out some sheets, pillows, a blanket, and even some towels. Mason didn't say anything; she hardly noticed he was there, except when she turned to make sure he was okay with her selection. He seemed relieved, only nodding and agreeing with whatever she suggested and following them around with the cart.

Somehow, bedsheet shopping turned to clothes shopping, and she helped Cassie with a few outfits too. By the time they finished, Mason's cart was overflowing.

"Looks like we did good," she said. "Right, Cassie?"

The girl giggled. "I can't see Daddy from behind the cart." She looked around to make sure that Mason indeed was behind the cart.

"Did you have fun, baby?" Mason asked as he looked around the mountain of stuff.

Cassie nodded. "'Melia's really good at picking colors and stuff."

"I'm glad to help. Now—oh no!" She realized that she had been so busy, she had abandoned her own cart.

"Your stuff," Mason said. "Sh—I mean, oh no. Sorry," he said sheepishly. "Let me go find it—"

"No, it's okay." She glanced around. "I'll go get it. You guys go ahead and pay." She ran off toward where she last saw her cart. Thankfully, it was still there, untouched. Amelia got behind it and pushed, then walked to the cashiers. It was Sunday and so it was quite crowded and she saw Mason up ahead of her. She got into the shortest line she found and waited.

Amelia sighed and gripped the cart's handle. What had she been thinking? Well, she wasn't. It wasn't like she was just going to breeze past Mason and Cassie when the child was obviously in distress and Mason was at his wit's end. Really, she should have done that, but she wasn't a stone-cold bitch. And, seeing Cassie's face light up as she talked and smiled made her feel better, too.

But she shouldn't be feeling this way. She needed to stay

away from Mason, not push her way into his life. He had made his choice long ago, that was obvious, and even if he was already divorced, it shouldn't matter. He currently had his hands full.

It seemed like she had waited forever, but finally, it was her turn. Mason and Cassie were probably long gone by now. The cashier rang her up and ran her credit card, and Amelia filled her cart with all her bags and headed out.

As soon as the doors slid open, she got the shock of her life. Mason, with Cassie in his arms, stood there, blocking her way. God, did the man not have any bad side? In his leather jacket, beanie, and white shirt—carrying a toddler, of all things—he looked even better, giving off that hot single dad vibe.

"Mason?" she asked. "I thought you'd left."

He gave her a sheepish smile. "Cassie wouldn't let us leave until she thanked you."

Cassie pouted. "It's not polite. I told Daddy that."

"You didn't have to wait for me," Amelia said as she pushed her cart out of the way to let the shoppers behind her through.

"She said it couldn't wait."

"And also, we should thank you by buying you dinner. Right, Daddy?"

"Right."

"There's no need for that, I didn't do anything," she insisted.

"You like tacos, right?" Cassie said. "Daddy said you love tacos and that one time you ate ten in one sitting."

Amelia went red. "You remembered," she whispered to Mason.

"Of course I did." He flashed her a smile that made her

heart flip-flop. "So, there's a taco place next door. We can help you load up, and then have dinner, then drive back to Blackstone. What do you say?"

"Pwease, 'Melia?" Cassie pleaded.

It was obvious what her answer would be. "All right." She grinned at Mason. "I never could resist tacos."

Dinner went as well as Amelia could hope for, or even better. She didn't know if having Cassie there as a buffer helped, but surprisingly, she didn't feel any awkwardness or unease being around Mason. He was attentive to Cassie, making sure she was okay, getting her a high chair and ordering for her. In fact, he was the perfect father, and Amelia couldn't help but admire him. Mason may have been a lying asshole, but it was obvious he cared for his daughter.

But she's not his daughter.

Amelia was still confused. But, if Mason wanted to go on pretending that Cassie was his, then it was none of her business.

"Wow!" Cassie exclaimed. "You really can eat ten tacos!"

Amelia smiled as she wiped her mouth with a napkin. "Girls can do anything, you know." Never mind that Mason ate twice as much as she did. "Did you like all the stuff you picked out for your bed?" she asked.

"Yeah!" She raised her fist in triumph. "And once we get the bed and my stuff set up, that mean dragon lady won't try to take me away."

"Mean dragon—" Amelia only knew of *one* dragon lady in town. What was going on?

Mason cleared his throat. "Cassie, baby. Looks like you

finished your plate, even your veggies." Mason reached over to release her from the high chair. "Why don't you go play in the kids section?" He nodded to the corner in the restaurant, which served as a play area for children.

"Yay!" Cassie, happy to be released from the constricting chair, ran off toward the play area.

"I owe you an explanation," Mason began as soon as Cassie was gone. He kept glancing over to where his daughter was playing, keeping an eye on her.

"You don't owe me anything," she said. "But I am curious as to why Cassie thinks Sybil's going to take her away from you."

"And you're probably wondering why she's human."

She shrugged. "Again, that's not my business."

He let out a sigh. "When I … went back to see Jenna, my CO and her uncle, Admiral Peters, 'encouraged' me to do the right thing," he scoffed. "And so, I married her."

Amelia felt her throat close. This wasn't what she wanted to hear right now, and she considered getting up and leaving, but when she looked at Cassie as she was on a rocking horse, the girl waved at her. She flashed her a tight smile back.

"I went back to my deployment after the wedding. Like, right after the ceremony. I was gone for months, not taking any leave. I couldn't stand her and what happened. Finally, I went back when Cassie was born." His eyes glinted like hard ice. "Jenna acted all normal, I knew something was wrong the moment I looked at Cassie. She didn't smell right."

Although most shifters didn't start turning into their animals until they were about three or four, it was always easy for a shifter to tell if a baby was one of theirs. The smell of fur or feathers was one sign, but generally, shifters had that immediate instinct that they could just *tell* if someone was a shifter or not.

"I confronted her right then and there. She didn't realize that I would be able to tell that Cassie wasn't mine."

Amelia's heart began to race. And she wanted to feel angry. She clenched her fists under the table as the implication of what he was saying was sinking in.

"I hated her. Hated everything. I ran, but my CO and the Admiral, plus Jenna's parents, came to me. They told me I had to do the right thing again. I told them to go stick it where the sun don't shine. I went back to get my things at the house and I wanted to just leave. But"—his eyes tracked back to Cassie, happily playing and oblivious to what was going on—"when I laid eyes on her again, I knew I had to do the right thing. Not for Jenna, but for her. Without me, Cassie would have been neglected and abused. But it happened anyway."

Her breath caught in her throat, and despite the maelstrom of emotions within her, Amelia managed to keep it together. "What happened?"

"Remember the other night at The Den, when I said I had to go?" She nodded. "That was CPS calling."

Mason relayed to her what had happened in the last couple of days. About Cassie's mom going on the run and abandoning her. Oh, rage was coursing through Amelia's veins all right. Rage towards that selfish bitch.

"And now, I need to get my act together before the social worker from the welfare office—Sybil—comes for her first home visit." He looked down at his empty plate, eyes somber.

"Sybil's strict, but fair," she said. She wanted to reach out and reassure him, but instead kept her hands in her lap. "You show her you're doing the best you can, and she'll understand."

"That's what Tim said, but that's just the first hurdle." Mason clasped his hands on the table. "I need to get a job—a real one—and then get someone to look after Cassie. Money won't be tight anymore, but I'm not swimming in it."

"Did you try to get a job at the mines? You know my brother—"

"That's why I didn't go," he confessed.

"Well, that's a stupid reason," she said, crossing her arms over her chest. "You're going to let the authorities take her away because of ..." Because what? Ben didn't know what happened to her or had even met Mason.

"Amelia ... about that. We need to talk about what happened four years ago. I wanted to tell you—"

"Daddy!" Cassie ran back to them, barreling into her father's arms. "Daddy, I'm tired. Can we go home now?" She lay her head on Mason's shoulder, her eyes struggling to stay open.

"Sounds like a great idea." Amelia's knees felt like jelly, but she managed to stand up. "I have an early day tomorrow. Cassie, I hope you like the bed sheets. I promise you, that dragon lady isn't mean at all. Thanks for the dinner, guys." She didn't dare look at Mason. The whole time, as she exited the restaurant, she could feel his stare, which only made her walk faster.

She made it to her car, managing to keep it together until she locked herself inside. When she was finally alone, she let out a sob, and she laid her head on the steering wheel.

All this time ... Mason didn't have to ... She couldn't think straight. There was a roaring in her ears that was deafening and the tears came harder. The icy feeling inside her broke, replaced with pure, white-hot rage.

But she wasn't mad at Mason or his mistakenly thinking

that Cassie would be his. No, the truth was, she would have respected him *less* if he didn't step up. He did what he thought was right at the time—the decent thing to do. Just like her dad did with Ben.

Amelia calmed herself, wiped the tears away, and started her car. Mason was getting his life back together, and so was she. She supposed Blackstone would be big enough for the both of them, and she could avoid them or at least pretend that nothing bothered her. Besides, what was she expecting? A happy ever after with Mason? He had a lot on his plate and she wasn't sure she could even feel anything again after what had happened.

She put the gear into drive, but before she could step on the gas, her phone rang. She frowned at the unfamiliar number. "Hello?"

"Amelia, are you okay?"

Mason? How did he ... *oh right*. She never changed her number. She deleted his, but apparently, he still had hers. "I'm fine." *Act normal.* "What's up?"

"I was trying to tell you—"

"Hey, you know what? I have a great idea!" She had to deflect the conversation. This was not happening. She didn't want to talk about what had happened four years ago. "For Cassie. Sybil will approve, I promise you."

"Oh. What's that?"

"Well, Lennox Corp. has this excellent day care facility. Super safe and Cassie can be around other kids. It's great, my cousin has his kid there."

"But I'm not an employee."

"You will be if you get a job at the mines. Mason, there's really no reason for you not to work there, if you need the job."

"You don't have to do me any favors," Mason said. "Not after—"

"Don't worry about it okay? I'll take care of it, and I'll have them call you. You won't even have to talk to Ben. Oops! My red light turned green, gotta go!" She hung up, heaved a sigh, then stepped on the gas, driving out of the parking lot.

Her grip tightened on the wheel. She wasn't sure why she offered to help. Ben wouldn't mind of course, especially if he knew Mason's circumstances and that he was Tim's nephew. She knew she didn't have to help him, in fact, anyone else in her position would have said "tough luck" and gone on their way.

"It's for Cassie," she said aloud, trying to convince herself.

CHAPTER EIGHT

MASON WALKED through the modern glass doors of The Lennox Corporation headquarters, located just at the edge of Blackstone. He waved to the receptionist as he walked by and the young woman returned the gesture, recognizing him. He headed straight to the elevators that took him to the second-floor day care facility.

It was hard to believe that two weeks had passed. There was still no word on Jenna and Doug. The detective on the case had given him an update, saying they suspected they had snuck across the border. But, Mason didn't give a fuck. Jenna and Doug could stay in Mexico, drink Mai Tais on the beach or whatever the fuck they want. He had Cassie, and that was all that mattered.

The one person who he did want to hear from, on the other hand, was nowhere to be seen. After that night at the restaurant, Amelia didn't call or message. He contemplated calling her, but the way she ran out at the restaurant, it was obvious she needed the space. He shouldn't have told her everything and there were still so many things left unspoken between them. Mason didn't want to hurt her more than he already had.

But, as she promised, someone called him and asked him to come in for an interview at the Blackstone mines.

Mason decided to swallow his pride, for Cassie's sake. As Amelia promised, he was interviewed by another manager, and not her brother. He started work the very next day, helping with the processing of the blackstone. He had yet to see the actual mining, as that part was reserved for the more senior employees. It was part-time for now, but it was work. Plus, he also worked the bar at The Den. Tim helped him find someone to look after Cassie during the evenings, an elderly wolf shifter lady who lived not far from their place. It was only on weekends and a couple hours, but it was extra money, so he couldn't say no. He was just glad he would have enough money to rent a two-bedroom apartment soon, possibly by the time Sybil Lennox came for her second home visit.

Just as Tim and Amelia had said, Sybil Lennox was firm, but fair. She came in, all business-like, and acted professionally. She was extra nice to Cassie, which he appreciated and treated Mason like they had never met before. She said everything seemed to be in order, but did say she would be making regular visits, at least for the next six months. For a moment, he thought he saw her face soften and even wished him good luck. It was probably because as Cassie's caseworker, she knew everything that had happened. He wasn't looking for sympathy, but he'd take them if it helped him score points with the she-dragon.

The elevator doors slid open and Mason walked toward the Lennox Day Care Center, signed in at the security desk, and then walked through the glass door when he heard the buzz.

The waiting room was empty, as it was still early. He wasn't working at the mines today, so he thought he'd sign Cassie out before five and have an early dinner before dropping her off at the babysitter's.

"Mason, how nice to see you." Irene, the woman in charge of the day care center, came out to greet him. "Cassie's just getting her things together. She'll be—"

The door buzzed behind him and they both turned. A tall, imposing man walked inside. He nodded at Irene, and then turned his tawny-golden gaze at Mason.

Mason reined in his polar bear as the other male sized him up. He felt the man do the same to his—tiger? lion?—and then gave him a nod. This was a day care, after all, not the African savanna.

"Luke," Irene said. "Are you checking out Grayson early too?"

"Yeah. Georgina's working late again, so I said I'd pick him up and feed him dinner."

"No worries," Irene said. "I'll go get him ready, too." With that, she turned and walked back into the main room.

"Do I know you?" Luke said when they were alone.

"Mason," he introduced himself.

"Are you new around here?" Golden eyes looked at him suspiciously.

"Yeah. I just moved here with my daughter. And you are?"

"Luke." He offered his hand and Mason took it with a firm shake. "Do you work here?"

"Not here. At the mines."

"Ah, I used to work there too," he explained. "I moved here. To the marketing department on the fifteenth floor."

Marketing? With his size, Luke Lennox looked like he should be a bouncer or a bodybuilder, not a marketing guy.

"Long story," Luke said, obviously sensing his confusion, but didn't offer any other explanation.

"Right." Everyone was entitled to their private business.

A few seconds of awkward silence passed.

"Army?" Luke finally said, his eyes on the tats on Mason's forearm.

"Navy," he corrected. "SEALs. Former."

"Really?" Luke rubbed his chin. "And you moved here to work at the mines?"

"Long story," he shot back, but grinned at the other man.

"Papa!"

"Daddy!"

Two small bundles of energy came out of the door where Irene had disappeared into.

"Hey, baby," Mason greeted as he kissed Cassie on the nose.

"You came early!" she giggled.

"Of course, I wanted to come and take you to dinner. I heard there was this place called Rosie's that had good pie."

"Rosie's?" came a voice from behind. "I love Rosie's! Can we go too, Papa?"

"Oh no, Grayson, we already went last Sunday. You should eat the dinner Momma made you."

"Aww!"

Mason turned around. A boy of around four or five stood next to Luke, holding his hand.

"Daddy, that's my friend, Grayson," Cassie said as Mason put her down on the floor. "He goes here to the day care, too."

"Hello, Grayson." Mason knelt down so he could be at eye

level with the boy. He narrowed his eyes at Grayson. He could have sworn he heard the boy call Luke "papa", but the boy wasn't a lion cub. He was a bear cub. Of course, maybe his wife was a bear.

"Hello, sir," he said in a small voice.

"Daddy, he's a bear, like you," Cassie proclaimed. "But my daddy's a polar bear."

Grayson nodded. "I'm a bear. My papa's a lion and Pop-pop is a dragon. Grams and Mommy are human, though."

Mason was confused. How many dragons were in Blackstone?

"I also know a dragon lady," Cassie said. "My daddy said she was mean, but 'Melia said was nice. She was right."

"Mean?" Luke asked, his voice rising slightly. "Sybil's not mean." He crossed his arms over his chest, and his gaze zeroed in on Mason. "Why would my sister be visiting *you*? And how do you know Amelia?"

Sister? Mason wasn't just confused. He was downright baffled.

"You know Auntie Sybil and Auntie Amelia?" Grayson said.

"Yeah, she took me shopping, and then Miss Sybil came to the house and asked me some questions." Cassie said. "They're your aunts?"

"Yeah. But Auntie Amelia's a bear, like me." Grayson's little brows furrowed together. "At least I think so. She's weird. She smells strange." Luke frowned at him in warning. "Oops! Papa says I'm not supposed to say that out loud. It's rude."

Mason's heart thudded in his chest at the child's words. He remembered how he made that observation when he saw Amelia again.

"Grayson, will you wait outside, please?" Luke said. "And why don't you take Cassie with you?"

"That means he wants to talk like adults," Grayson stage-whispered to Cassie. "Okay Papa!" He took Cassie's hand and led her outside of the waiting area.

When the kids were gone, Luke turned to Mason. "I remember you. You're related to Tim. You came to visit a few years ago." Tawny eyes pierced right into him, as if daring him to lie.

"Yeah. So?"

"You were sniffing around her, weren't you? I thought you looked familiar." Luke crossed his arms over his chest. "I know it's none of my business, but Amelia is my family. Something happened to her that made her leave. She didn't come back the same."

The broken mating bond. Luke had noticed it, then maybe it was true. Was Amelia sick because of what he did? If so, then he would never forgive himself.

"She's mine." *Was min*e, he corrected himself. "But it didn't work out back then."

"Are you going to get her back?" Luke glared at him.

He sighed. "I ... She's been avoiding me. Besides, I have Cassie to think about."

"You do," he said. "But just because you've got a kid, doesn't mean you can't have a mate."

"Is she sick?"

Luke shook his head. "She's not the same, I can tell you that. But I never asked. Maybe I should have. Listen," Luke began. "If you showed up around here months ago, I would have kicked your ass and told you stay the hell away from her."

Mason snorted.

"But, if she's yours and you're hers, then you should fix things between you. Believe me, nothing good will come from denying your animals." Luke shoved his hands in his pockets. "I gotta go take my son home. And your kid is probably starving too, though she's got a human's appetite, I imagine, something you should be thankful for."

"Ha."

"If you want to fix it, then do it soon," Luke said before he turned away.

Mason stared after Luke. He didn't know the man, but he was right. Cassie was always going to need him, and he would always care for her. But, if something was wrong with Amelia, he would have to fix it now, before it was too late.

Mason couldn't sleep. Not after what Luke had told him. He played the events over and over again in his mind. And each time, he only came to the same conclusion: he broke her somehow. It was dawn when he decided that it was up to him to fix her.

He got Cassie ready for day care, dropped her off, and then went to work at the mines. It was a good thing that they finished work early, so he was already outside the building where Amelia worked at four that afternoon. He waited across the street, counting the minutes until five.

Sure enough, ten minutes after five, Amelia breezed out of the building. She was dressed in her usual office attire—jacket, blouse, pencil skirt, and sensible heels. Her dark blonde hair was tied into a bun at the nape of her neck.

Mine! His polar bear roared when he set eyes on her. How

could he not realize what his bear had been telling him all these years?

She walked east, to the small lot a block away where he knew she had parked. Using his shifter speed, he quickly got in front of her.

"Mason?" she asked. "What are you doing here?"

"I'm sorry," he said.

"For what—Mason!"

He grabbed her arm and pulled her into the empty alleyway beside her building. He pushed her against the wall and leaned forward.

She placed her hands on his chest to push him away. She was strong, but he was stronger. He slammed his palms on either side of her, trapping her, and moved in closer, trying to catch her scent. Mint shampoo. Traces of ink and paper. Sweat. But he couldn't pick up her scent of fur and honeysuckle. He tipped her head up toward him and looked straight into her eyes. What he saw there—or didn't—would haunt him forever. It was like staring into an empty void.

"Amelia?"

"Get away from me." Her voice was quiet, but dead serious.

"No," he said. "Not until you tell me what's going on. Why do you smell like this? Is your bear sick?" His own animal whimpered, unable to feel its mate, and pain slashed through him.

"It's none of your business. Now, please." She swallowed hard. "Let me go."

"I can't," he rasped. "Please, Amelia. Tell me what happened."

"I ..." She broke into a sob, and his stomach dropped like a stone. "It's gone. My bear. It's just ... vanished."

"It's my fault." Mason knew it. Amelia's silence and her

refusal to meet his eyes told him it was true. "You were trying to tell me we had bonded. I didn't understand. But I should have." He pulled away from her, then slammed his fist against the wall so hard that the cement broke under his fingers. The sound of breaking bones was unmistakable too, and made her jump in surprise. "I broke you. I broke us."

He deserved to die. And his polar bear agreed. It roared so loudly, his ears rang. He could feel the rage and hate flowing through him. His fingers were growing, turning into claws. Fur sprouted on his arms. His teeth pierce at his lips as they began to elongate.

"Stop!" Amelia cried. "Please. Stop."

Mason's bear roared, the sound inhuman and feral. *I'm sorry*! Mason screamed from deep inside. The animal growled. When it looked at Amelia, at the real fear in her eyes, it whimpered and slowly began to back away. Half transformed, Mason braced himself against the wall, his claws digging into the cement as he sank to his knees.

A few heartbeats passed. "Mason?" Amelia said in a quiet voice.

Mason gnashed his teeth together and slowly got up. He knew what he had to do. "I'm going to fix you," he vowed. "I don't care how long it takes."

She sighed. "You can't. I can't be fixed. Don't you think I've tried?" Amelia asked. "I've searched the Internet for answers, tried asking other shifters … I haven't found anything."

Mason raked his fingers through his hair. "There's never been a case like this before, where a shifter just loses his animal. They might go crazy or feral, but to totally disappear? I don't accept it. I *can't*."

She shrugged. "I have. Look, Mason, it's all in the past. I've come to terms with what happened."

Mason felt hope slipping away. "There must be something we can do. We can go to the woods and try to get you in touch with your bear again. Or go to a therapist."

"I've tried all that," Amelia said. "I moved away because I thought it would fix things. And there aren't any shifter therapists specializing in this kind of thing. I've looked all over the world. No one can help me." She turned away.

He placed a hand on her shoulder. "I'm going to try."

"You have a child, Mason. Cassie needs you." Amelia shrugged his hand away. "You can't fix me and take care of her, too."

"I love Cassie with all my heart and soul. But I wronged you, and I have to make it right."

"You don't have to."

His bear disagreed. It wanted Mason to fix it. *Now.* "I can—"

"No." She put a hand up. "Please, Mason, I've come to terms with this. Life moves on. *I've* moved on."

The words were like a knife, cutting into his heart. While Amelia may have moved on, he had to face facts: he had *not* moved on. "Amelia—"

"No more. Please, just leave it be." Her voice trembled, but her face remained impassive. "There's nothing anyone can do. Just leave it alone." She sighed. "I'm tired and I want to go home."

He didn't move a muscle. "All right then."

She opened her mouth, then closed it again. She gave him a nod, and then turned on her heel.

Mason watched as Amelia walked out of the alleyway. He knew he should respect her wishes, but at the same time, the need to help her was too strong. He'd gone through some shit in his life, but the hollow, empty look in Amelia's eyes was the worst thing he'd ever seen.

I have to fix things. And he had an idea how. Whether Amelia would agree to his plan was the question.

If a broken bond made her bear go away, then maybe fixing the bond would bring it back.

CHAPTER NINE

"Everything okay, Amelia?" Erin asked.

"Huh?" She looked up at Erin. "Yeah, I'm good. Why do you ask?"

Her boss leaned her hip against the desk. "You've been staring at that for hours."

Amelia followed Erin's gaze, leading her to the empty sheet of paper on the table. "Oh. Sorry, I'm just … I have a lot of things on my mind."

"It's okay, I know it's hard to be creative just like that." Erin snapped her fingers for emphasis. "Why don't you go home? You can start again tomorrow."

"T-thanks. And, sorry." Amelia really was embarrassed, having been caught by her boss in a daze.

"Don't worry. Go home, have a glass of wine, work on your apartment." She and Erin had been chatting about how she was decorating her new house.

"I do have boxes to unpack."

"Go." Erin waved her away. "Work will still be here tomorrow."

Amelia didn't argue with her boss, and instead grabbed her things. "Thanks Erin. I'll see you tomorrow."

As she walked out of the office and to the elevator, she kept her guard up. Sure, it was unlikely Mason would be waiting for her again, but she couldn't help herself. She was surprised at his sudden appearance yesterday, and even more shocked at what had transpired. She had become so good at keeping up appearances, she never thought anyone would figure out what she'd been hiding, much less him. She should have been more careful, but there was nothing she could do about it now.

Still, she was curious. How did he figure it out? What did he see that told him something was wrong?

Amelia sighed. No use thinking about it now. She put it out of her head, walked to the lot where she'd parked her car, and drove home.

The house she rented was all the way across town, but she didn't care. Blackstone wasn't too big and there was hardly any traffic, so she pulled into her driveway about fifteen minutes later. While she wanted to take Erin's advice and have a glass of wine, she really did have boxes to unpack. Said boxes greeted her as she opened the door. With a great big sigh, she put her things down, took her heels off, and got to work. She tackled the boxes one by one, putting stuff away, until there was one box left.

This box contained all her oldest stuff; some memories and keepsakes from her childhood and high school. She ripped the top open and began to unpack the various knick-knacks—her yearbook, photos of her family and friends, an old stuffed wolf she used to bring around. When she picked up an old sketch book, something fluttered to the ground and she picked it up.

Amelia held her breath as she looked at the old napkin with the sketch of a house done in red ink. *I kept this?* The memory of that day was still clear in her mind.

She had been waiting for Mason at that hipster diner in Verona Mills. He was running late, doing an errand for Tim, so to pass the time, she started drawing. She'd dreamt of the house just a few nights ago and had been itching to get it down on paper. It was a big, beautiful cabin, much like her dad's and Ben's, though she liked to think she'd improved it with a modern flair, like the sunken living room, big glass windows and skylights, and clean, straight lines. She had also imagined at least four bedrooms for the kids and a big master bedroom for herself and Mason.

Amelia swallowed the lump in her throat. She had been planning that house for them, for the family they would have. She should have known it was too soon, but she had been young and foolish, thinking that being mates would automatically mean a happy ever after.

A ringing sound startled her, and she lunged for her phone on the coffee table.

"Amelia?"

"I—Mason?" Why was he calling?

He let out a breath. "Amelia, I'm sorry for calling last minute, but I'm kind of in a bind."

"Is it Cassie?" she asked, concern creeping in.

"Yeah. I have to work at The Den. One of the waitresses broke her leg. Tim asked if I could fill in, and I couldn't say no. I called Cassie's usual sitter, but she's out. I got no one to watch her. I could take her to work, but ..."

"Oh." Take Cassie to The Den? Was he serious? She shook her head. *Men.* "Do you need me to come over?"

"Would you mind?" he asked, sounding unsure. "You were great with her and I don't have anyone else."

"Of course, I'll be right over."

"Thanks. I'll text you the address." He hung up before she could change her mind. A few seconds later, a message came in with the location of his apartment.

Amelia knew she should have said no, but he sounded desperate. Plus, it wasn't like she would be spending time with Mason. No, he would be at work and she would just be with Cassie.

Mason didn't specify the time, but he sounded like he needed her to be there right away. She got her purse, stuffed her phone inside, and looked around her. She grabbed a couple more things and was soon on her way.

Twenty minutes later, Amelia found herself outside Mason's apartment. It was too late to back out now, so she knocked on the door. A few seconds later, it swung open.

"I brought art supplies," she said, holding up a canvas bag. "I didn't know what Cassie liked to do."

Mason's eyes lit up. "I'm sure it's fine. I have some toys and games." He opened the door to let her in. "Sorry, it's not much." He looked almost embarrassed as he glanced around at his apartment.

Amelia looked around. The studio was small, but clean. There was a futon in the middle of the room, a small table and two chairs, and a lamp. In the corner was a child's bed, which was made up with all the sheets and pillows they had bought at the store. "It's fine," she said. "Very cozy."

"Let me help you with that," Mason said, grabbing the bags. He placed them on top of the futon.

"'Melia! 'Melia!" Cassie ran into her legs, nearly knocking her over. "You came."

"Of course I did." She bent down to her level. It had seemed like ages since she last saw Cassie. She brushed her hair away from her face. "I wasn't going to leave you alone."

"I'm glad." She wrapped her small arms around Amelia's neck and squeezed.

"Me too," she whispered in the girl's ear.

"Thank you for coming on such short notice."

Amelia stood up and faced Mason. "I didn't have any plans or anything. Besides, I wasn't going to let you take a little girl to a bar," she laughed.

"I appreciate it." He glanced at his watch, and then the door. "Tim's waiting."

She waved him away. "Go," she urged. "I'll take care of things here. Has she had dinner?"

Mason nodded. "Fridge is stocked if she's hungry, but no sweets."

"Daddy!" Cassie whined.

Amelia chuckled. "We'll be fine."

Mason leaned down and kissed Cassie on the cheek. "Be good, baby,"

"I will, Daddy."

He gave her another grateful nod. "I'll be back as soon as I can. I'm only across the street if you need me and you have my number."

"I know."

He ruffled Cassie's hair, and then headed out the door.

"Now," she looked down at Cassie. "Do you want to draw? I brought some paper and markers."

"Oohhh! I can't draw too good yet, but I can color," Cassie declared.

"Well, why don't I draw for you and you can color?"

Amelia found it easy to keep Cassie entertained. Although she hadn't any experience watching over kids, it seemed easy enough. Cassie was talkative, eager, and very bright. She was also very affectionate, always touching Amelia and hugging her. And Amelia couldn't help but return the affection. After four years of being alone, it felt good to have some contact, even if it was from a little girl.

The hours passed, and they watched movies, played some board games, and Cassie colored about twenty of her drawings. Amelia realized that Mason didn't tell her what Cassie's bedtime was, but it was nine o'clock and Amelia was pretty sure that was already way too late for a three-year-old.

"I think it's time for bed," she declared.

"Awww!"

Amelia put on her best stern face. "C'mon young lady. Let's get you ready." She helped Cassie wash her face, brush her teeth and get into her pajamas. "Want me to tuck you in?"

Cassie nodded. "But I'm not sleepy," she protested.

"Get into bed, while I turn down the lights." Amelia turned off the lights in the room, except for the lamp by the futon. She knelt down beside Cassie's bed. She had pulled the covers away and was lying down in the middle.

"Will you tell me a story, 'Melia?"

She wrinkled her nose. "A story? What kind? A princess story?"

Cassie shook her head. "No. I don't like princesses."

"Right," she chuckled. "What story do you want then?"

"Something with a bear," Cassie said. "And a dragon."

"Ah, you're in luck, because I happen to know a story

about a dragon and bear." Amelia pulled the covers over Cassie's shoulders. "Once upon a time, there was bear shifter. His name was Silas. Silas lived deep in the forest, all by himself."

"Why?" A small wrinkle appeared between Cassie's brows. "Why?"

"Why did he live by himself? Didn't he have other bears like him? Like Daddy?"

"Well…" Amelia paused. "Silas did have a family. A big bear family. But he was just … different. All his brothers, sisters, and cousins found their mates and he was the last of his family without one."

"What's a mate? Is that like a wife?"

"Yes, it's kind of like that," Amelia explained. "So, since Silas couldn't find a girl bear to be his mate, he thought he would just live in the woods alone for the rest of his days. He built a cabin by a lake, and spent his days hiking, hunting, and fishing. One day, Silas was out fishing when he saw a great big shadow over him. When he looked up, he saw it was a dragon."

"Was it a scary dragon?" Cassie clutched the blanket to her chest.

"Maybe. I'm sure Silas was scared to see the dragon; he'd never seen one before. But, the dragon was hurt. It had this great big tear in its wing and it fell in the lake. Silas dove into the lake and rescued the dragon, who turned out to be a girl."

Cassie looked at her with a skeptical face. "Was it a princess dragon?"

"I told you there weren't any princesses in this story," Amelia reminded her. "Anyway, Silas rescued her and brought her onto the shore. He laid her down on the ground and tried to wake her up. He breathed air into her, to get the water out of her lungs and she woke up. The moment he looked into her eyes, he knew that she was his mate."

"How did he know?"

"His bear told him. And her dragon told her too, that Silas was *her* mate."

"Did they get married?"

Amelia shook her head. "Not right away. Anastasia was very sick. She couldn't fly or turn back into a dragon. Silas nursed her back to health, until she was able to change back into a dragon and fly away."

"And did she?"

"Did she what?"

"Fly away?"

Amelia nodded. "She did. And Silas was very sad. He loved Anastasia, but she had to go home to her family. You see, dragons aren't supposed to have mates who aren't dragons, and Anastasia's family wanted her to marry this other dragon. A prince."

"A prince dragon?" Cassie made a face. "But I don't want her to be a dragon princess."

"Don't worry," Amelia assured her. "Anastasia loved Silas too, you see. She told her family that she didn't want to marry the dragon prince, and she ran away again, back to Silas. And—"

"They lived happily ever after?" Cassie asked, hope in her eyes.

She smiled down at the girl. "Of course they did."

Cassie let out a yawn. "I'm glad. I wouldn't want Silas to be alone." She blinked. "Like my daddy. I think he's lonely, too."

Amelia gave her a tight smile. "He has you, he'll never be alone."

"I know that." Another yawn. "But he needs a mate, right?"

"I—I guess."

"He does. And ..." She let out another yawn. "You ..." Cassie fought sleep for just a second, but then closed her eyes.

Amelia leaned down and pressed her nose to Cassie's cheek, memorizing her scent. Strawberries—probably from the bath gel she saw in the bathroom—and that fresh and sweet scent only kids had. She brushed her hair aside, and then tucked the covers around her, waiting until her breath evened and she was fast asleep.

She stood up and looked around her, realizing that there wasn't anywhere else for her to relax on except the futon. Mason's bed. She could sit on the chairs by the table or the floor, but her body felt so heavy and tired. Trudging over to the futon, she sat down, took off her shoes, and then lay on the mattress.

As she took a deep breath, she found herself surrounded by Mason's fur and fresh mountain air scent. She groaned and rolled onto her stomach. That made it worse as now her nose was buried in his pillow. But her body refused to move.

As she lay there, surrounded by Mason's scent, her mind drifted back to the story of Silas Walker and Anastasia Lennox. It had been a long time since she'd thought about that story; it had been her favorite growing up, and her dad would tell it to her at least once a week. Amelia always imagined she would one day tell it to her kids, so they would know all about their family history.

She sighed, her eyelids drooping until she just couldn't fight it anymore, and she closed them. She was slowly sinking into sleep when she felt something move beside her. The scent of strawberries told her it was Cassie, who had somehow crawled into bed with her.

Amelia moved over to give her some room. Cassie snuggled up to her, laying her head on her chest and wrapping her small hand around a lock of her hair. Amelia pulled her close, throwing an arm over the small body.

Just before sleep claimed her, Amelia thought she heard the sound of a deep, satisfied rumble.

CHAPTER TEN

As soon as Tim told him he could go, Mason didn't waste any time and ran back to his apartment. His uncle really had been in a bind, with Heather breaking her leg. Tim had said he could manage, but Mason wanted to help out.

Of course, Mason would be lying if he said he wasn't happy about how things turned out. It was the perfect excuse to call Amelia and see her, even just for a few minutes. He still hadn't worked out how he was going to fix her and the mating bond, but he just needed an opportunity or an excuse to spend time with her. Plus, he already knew she wouldn't be able to say no if it was Cassie. It was kind of a dick move, using his daughter, but he was desperate.

His animal had been on a rampage, ever since that day he discovered what Amelia was hiding. It had been so bad that his manager at the mines asked him to go home, since he was making all the other shifters agitated. He knew he had to fix this, or else he might go mad and feral himself.

Mason jogged up the stairs and opened the front door with his key. The room was dark, save for the lamp by the bedside, so he didn't bother to turn on any of the lights. As his eyes adjusted to the dim light, the sight that greeted him took his breath away.

Curled up on his futon were Amelia and Cassie. His daughter was cuddled up to Amelia, who was lying on her side. She had an arm protectively over Cassie, and both were fast asleep.

A tightness in his chest made it hard to breathe. *This is how it should have been.* But Mason quickly put those thoughts away. If he played it right, this is how it could always be.

Mason walked over to Cassie's side as quietly as he could, then knelt down. Amelia looked so peaceful and beautiful like this, her eyelids closed and mouth slightly parted. He reached over to brush her cheek with his hand.

"Shh," he said as her lids fluttered open. Sleepy blue eyes looked up at him. "I'll put her back in bed." He lifted Cassie into his arms, and though she stirred, she didn't wake up, even when he tucked her in. When he turned around, he saw Amelia had sat up and was putting her shoes on.

"Thanks again," he said as he walked over to her. "You really saved my butt."

"You're welcome." As she stood up, she lost her footing and toppled back.

Mason's reflexes kicked in and he snaked an arm around her waist. He was a little too forceful, so ended up with her body pressed to his. He stifled a groan at the feel of her soft curves.

"Mason?" Blue eyes blinked at him.

"Yes?"

"You can let go now."

"Oh." He dropped his arm. "Right." She was still so close though that he could almost feel the warmth of her skin.

"I should get going. I have work tomorrow."

"Yeah, sorry to keep you."

She glanced over at Cassie. "No worries. I'm glad I could help out. She's a good kid."

"She is."

Amelia made a grab for her purse, which was sitting on top of the futon. Unfortunately, he didn't move out of the way quickly enough, and she swung the bag and hit him in the chest.

"Oops!" She let go of the bag and it fell to the floor with a soft thud, the contents spilling out. "Damn."

He bent down. "I'll get it, no worries." As he picked up her stuff, he noticed a wadded up piece of paper on the floor. It was old and crumpled, covered in red ink. His fingers trembled when he picked it up. He got up and handed Amelia her purse, tucking the napkin into his pocket. "Here you go."

"Thanks." She slung it over his shoulder. "I'll head out now."

"I'll take you to your car."

"No," she said quickly. "I mean," she looked at Cassie, "you shouldn't leave her alone here, even for a few minutes. She shouldn't wake up to an empty house. My car's right outside."

He nodded in agreement but walked her to the door. "Good night, Amelia."

"Good night, Mason." And with that, she left.

Mason stared at the door for a few seconds, then turned and walked back to his futon. He took his boots off and stretched out on the bed, then took the napkin out from his pocket.

The drawing was just as he remembered, if a little faded. He remembered as she lovingly traced the lines with her ink-stained fingers, describing the dream home she had envisioned. He was surprised that she kept it all this time. Maybe they weren't a lost cause; maybe, just maybe, Amelia still held onto the past and the feelings she used to have. He refused to think it was all gone, and this was proof, right in his hands.

He looked at it for a few more minutes, then tucked it back into his pocket. He rolled over and closed his eyes, letting the exhaustion and sleep take over as the smell of honeysuckle and fur followed him into his dreams.

"Where are we going, Daddy?" Cassie asked as he unbuckled her from the car seat.

"We're going to see Amelia," he explained, then lifted her out.

Cassie's face lit up into a smile. "We are? Yay! I'm glad you took me out of day care early."

Mason grinned at his daughter. Cassie had been legitimately sad when he'd arrived early to pick her up. She really did enjoy staying at Lennox day care facility, and being the newest and youngest girl there, she was kind of a celebrity. All the other kids watched out for her and wanted to play with her. Of course, Cassie was such an extroverted and happy child, it wasn't a surprise. Mason himself realized that he'd never spent an extended period of time around his daughter and was slowly discovering her personality. She wasn't a perfect little girl and she had her bratty moments, but Mason loved her even more.

"Is 'Melia going to babysit me again?" Cassie asked.

Mason locked the doors to the truck. "No, baby. We're going to thank her for last night by taking her out to dinner." He cleared his throat. "You'll have to help me convince her to come, though. She might be too, er, shy to let us buy her dinner again."

"I will, Daddy."

With Cassie still in his arms, he walked across the street to Amelia's office building. He didn't have to wait long, as Amelia soon came out.

"Mason? Cassie?" she asked, her brow wrinkling.

"'Melia!" Cassie cried. "We're taking you to dinner!"

"Is that so?" Amelia raised a brow at Mason. "I don't recall being asked."

"It's a thank you dinner," Mason said.

"Like when you helped me with shopping and ate the tacos," Cassie pointed out. "Pwease, 'Melia?" Mason had to hand it to her, his daughter was laying it on thick with the big eyes and pleading look.

Amelia bit her lip, but there was a smile curling up at the corners. "All right. But, where should we go?"

"I want Rosie's!" Cassie exclaimed. "Daddy and me have only been once."

"That's my favorite place! I used to go with my parents and my brother." Amelia looked at Mason. "I'm good if you are."

Mason nodded. "Okay, let's go."

"I'll meet you there," Amelia said, fishing her car keys from her pocket. "See you."

Mason watched her walk toward the parking lot, and then ruffled Cassie's hair.

"Did I do good, Daddy?"

He chuckled. "You did more than good, baby. Let's go."

They went back to the truck and were soon on their way. Mason drove past the lot where Amelia parked and waited. When he saw her car pull out of the lot, he followed right behind her.

Rosie's Bakery and Cafe wasn't too far from where they were and they arrived there in less than ten minutes. He followed Amelia to the lot behind the cafe and parked right beside her.

"Let's go!" Cassie said as soon as Mason set her on the ground. She immediately ran to Amelia and took her hand. "I want chocolate mud pie!"

"Only after you've have your veggies," Amelia said with a wag of her finger.

"Aww!"

Rosie's wasn't packed yet when they entered, but there was one other couple waiting for a table by the hostess stand. The man had his back to him, but Mason could see he was very tall and built like a linebacker. He had an arm around a petite, redhead who was obviously very pregnant.

"Ben?" Amelia said, and the man turned around.

"Amelia!" He greeted, and then pulled her in for a hug. Mason's polar bear growled instinctively, but when he got a whiff of grizzly, he instantly knew who this was.

"Penny!" Amelia embraced the short redhead. "What are you doing here?"

The woman rubbed her tummy. "I think the baby's definitely taking after your brother. He or she wants Rosie's all the time." She chuckled, then glanced at Mason and Cassie. "Oh, hello."

Ben's gaze turned to Mason. "I didn't realize you weren't alone, Amelia." He kept his gaze straight at him, and Mason could feel the power of the grizzly inside Ben. Controlled, but it was difficult to ignore. It reminded him of the first time he met Amelia.

"Oh, yeah." Amelia's eyes darted around. "Ben, this is

Mason Grimes and his daughter, Cassie. Mason, Cassie, this is my brother, Ben, and his wife, Penny."

"How do you do?" Penny greeted.

"Grimes?" Ben said, his brows drawing together.

"Tim's my uncle," Mason explained.

"Oh. I didn't realize Tim had other relatives." He offered his hand. "Nice to meet you."

"Same." Mason took his hand and gripped it tight. Their bears seemed to size each other up, but with the women and Cassie around, both backed down from any type of confrontation.

"Excuse me—Oh, Ben! Amelia!" Rosie, the owner of the cafe, exclaimed. "How nice to see you both together. So, just one table for all of you?"

"Why not," Penny said. "You've been back in town for a couple of weeks, but we've hardly seen you."

Amelia looked at Mason. "Of course," he said. Mason glanced at Ben from the corner of his eye as Rosie led them to their table. He wondered if Ben knew anything about what happened four years ago. *Probably not.* If he did, Mason suspected that he'd be at the opposite end of teeth and claws, not having a nice dinner at Rosie's.

CHAPTER ELEVEN

Rosie sat them at a big table in the middle of the dining room. Mason put Cassie in a high chair between Amelia and himself, while Ben and Penny sat across from them. They quickly ordered and Rosie promised to return with their drinks.

"Nice to bump into you here," Ben said.

"Of course." Amelia really was glad to see her brother and his mate, though she knew Ben would have many questions. She just hoped it wouldn't get too awkward.

"You must be really busy," Penny said. "We've only seen you once since you got here."

"Yeah, well I have a new job, new house—"

"New friend?" Ben looked meaningfully at Mason.

"Actually, we're old friends," Mason said. "Just reconnecting."

"I see."

Thankfully, Rosie did come back as she promised with the drinks they ordered. Rosie hung around and asked Penny about the baby and how she was feeling. Amelia was glad for the distraction, though it was hard to ignore the way Ben kept glancing over at Mason. To his credit, Mason did his best to ignore her brother, focusing on Cassie instead and trying to get her to drink her milk. When Rosie left, Amelia immediately took control of the conversation, asking Ben about the nursery, which of course, distracted her brother enough, at least, until Rosie came back with their food.

"So, how did you two meet? How many years ago?" Ben asked when Rosie left their table. "Are you visiting or staying here in Blackstone?"

"Ben." Penny rolled her eyes, and then turned to Cassie. "How old are you, sweetie?"

"I'm three," Cassie proclaimed as she dug into her beef pot pie.

"Do you like the pie?" Amelia asked.

Cassie nodded. "It's good." She looked at Amelia's half-finished plate. "Don't you like it, 'Melia?"

"I'm just not hungry right now," she said. In truth, she'd been too anxious having her brother and Mason at the same table that she hardly noticed her food.

"Maybe Daddy can get you more tacos after we finish here. I'm sure you could eat at least ten more."

"She does love her tacos," Ben said with a laugh. "Do you go out to dinner often?"

"Ben," Penny warned again, placing a hand on Ben's arm.

"What?" He smiled innocently at Amelia. "They're *friends*, right?"

"We always take 'Melia to dinner to say thank you," Cassie interjected.

"For what, sweetie?" Penny asked.

"Well ..." Cassie tapped a finger on her chin and cocked her head. "The first time was when she helped me pick out my sheets. Green is my favorite color and she got the best ones. And then last night, 'Melia slept in Daddy's bed."

"Cassie!" Mason dropped his fork so quickly, it made a clattering sound as it hit the plate.

Penny's jaw dropped and Amelia spit out the water she was drinking. Ben's expression was inscrutable, but there was an unmistakable glow that signaled his bear was lurking at the surface.

"I ... was ... babysitting." Amelia cleared her throat of the water that had gone down the wrong pipe, then wiped her mouth and the table. "Mason had to work at The Den. Someone broke their leg and he was filling in."

"Heather," Penny said. When Mason looked at her, she added, "I'm the waitress on maternity leave. She texted me yesterday, telling me about how she fell off a ladder."

Ben's face and eyes returned to normal. "And you were sleeping in his bed because ..."

"I was watching over Cassie," Amelia continued. "And I fell asleep because Mason didn't come back until after midnight."

Penny looked up at Ben. "Amelia was doing her friend a favor, and now he's thanking her. Isn't that right?"

Mason nodded. "I just want to be a good friend."

Amelia wanted to strangle the next person who said *friend*. For some reason, the word annoyed her right now, especially when referring to Mason. She was about to berate Ben for overreacting when Cassie spoke up.

"Daddy, Daddy, I gotta go potty."

Mason stood up. "Okay baby, I got you."

"I should go too," Penny said, putting her napkin on the table. "I swear, my bladder's the size of a pea these days."

"Maybe Penny can help you," Amelia said.

"But I want Daddy," Cassie insisted.

"It's okay." Mason looked at Amelia and Penny. "I just usually stand outside the door while she does her business." He unbuckled Cassie from the high chair and set her down.

"We'll be back," Penny declared as she followed Mason and Cassie to the ladies' room.

"So," Ben said when they were alone. "Anything you want to tell your big brother? I know I'm seeing something going on here. Should I bring out the shovel?"

Amelia pushed her plate at him. "Here, have mine. I heard hunger can make people see things."

"Amelia," Ben said, his voice turning serious. "I'm not stupid; I can see the way Mason looks at you."

"It's nothing." She waved a hand at him. "I'm not interested."

"Is it because of that kid?" Ben asked. "You're not interested because of his baggage?"

"What?" Her voice rose, and a roar of denial came from somewhere deep in her. "No! Cassie's not baggage, don't say that." Her hands gripped the edge of the table.

"Whoa there, she-bear," Ben teased, raising his hands. "I'm not saying anything. She seems like a good kid." He chuckled. "Probably going to be a troublemaker someday. So, is she like, a niece or something? Adopted?"

Ben must have sensed that Cassie was human but was too polite to say anything. Amelia sighed. "Well, it's complicated, but …" She quickly told him the story, telling him only the pertinent details.

"Whoa." Ben's face was one of disbelief. "I …" He shook his head and rubbed the back of his neck with his palm. "That's some serious shit he's got going on."

"Tell me about it." Which is why Mason didn't need

another burden. That's what she was trying to tell him the other day when he said he was going to fix her.

"But, I can't help but feel respect for him. He sounds like a good man."

Amelia knew that her brother had been thinking of his own situation, when he was a kid, and she couldn't help but feel her heart swell. Yes, Mason really was a good man, stepping up like that when he didn't even have to, when Cassie wasn't even his own flesh and blood. Knowing that her brother approved of him made her feel warm inside.

Ben's expression changed. "Everything okay?"

Penny had come back and sat on the chair beside him. "Yup. Good as gold."

Mason put Cassie back in her chair, and then sat down. "What'd we miss?"

Amelia looked at Ben and smiled.

The rest of the dinner proceeded with no more awkward questions. It was like something had changed, and Amelia was glad her brother wasn't quite as suspicious as he was at the beginning. She felt a little guilty about telling him Mason's private business, but she knew Ben might have asked questions, which would have led to more awkwardness. She didn't know what Mason told Cassie or what his plans were for what to say to his daughter when she grew up and realized she was different. Surely, being surrounded by shifters, Cassie would eventually figure it out.

When they finished and Rosie brought the check, Ben insisted on paying. "No buts," he said. "I don't always get to see my sister and meet new friends." He winked at Cassie.

"Thank you," Mason said. "Cassie…"

"Thank you for dinner!" The girl said as Mason took her out of the chair.

Ben smiled at Cassie. "And thank you for being good company."

"We had a great time," Penny added.

Ben turned to Mason. "Why didn't you tell me you worked at the mines? Stop by my office anytime if you need anything. I usually try to go home to Penny for lunch, but I'm mostly there the whole day until three."

"I'll do that," Mason said as they clasped hands. "Thanks."

Ben and Penny waved goodbye as they walked away and so Amelia found herself alone with Mason and Cassie once again. "Thanks for taking me to dinner," she said as they walked back to the parking lot. Cassie was between them, holding their hands.

"Technically, your brother got us dinner," Mason pointed out.

"Well, you still invited me."

"I think that means Cassie and I owe you," he said, his eyes dancing with mischief. "How about dinner tomorrow?"

Amelia stopped in her tracks. "Mason, this really isn't—"

"'Melia!" Cassie cried, the distress in her voice obvious. "What happened to your car?"

Amelia's head whipped around toward her parking spot. Her car was still there, but it was trashed—the tires had been slashed, the windows smashed in, and scratches ran up and down the sides. Her heart stopped and her blood turned to ice. "What the …" She made a step toward her car, but Mason blocked her. "I need to check—"

"Stop." Mason's voice was almost inhuman. "Go back inside, Amelia, and take Cassie with you."

She put her hands on her hips. "Mason, you're being ridic—"

Eyes like twin blue shards of glass pierced into her. "I said go."

Amelia felt the hair on the back of her neck stand on end at the cold, deadly expression on his face. *He was worried for Cassie*, she told herself. With a nod, she picked up a confused Cassie and jogged back into Rosie's.

"Did you forget something?" Rosie asked when they walked in again.

"No." Amelia shook her head. "It's ... someone vandalized my car."

"What?" Rosie's eyes grew wide as saucers. "Are you okay? Did you see who did it? Did—"

The door slamming open made both women startle. Mason came in, fury obvious in his face and the way his body tensed. His eyes were an eerie luminous blue. "Do you have cameras out there?" he asked Rosie.

The proprietress shook her head. "I'm afraid the security company hasn't put them back yet, not after the incident a couple of weeks ago."

Mason let out a grunt, then turned to Amelia. "We need to call the police. And get you some protection."

"Police ... protection?" *Was he crazy?* "Mason you're over-reacting. I'm sure it was just some kids. Maybe a prank."

"That didn't look like a prank." Mason's hands turned into fists at his sides. "My truck doesn't have a scratch on it, nor does any other car in the lot. They were targeting *you*."

"Me? Mason, that just means it really was just a prank. Maybe some kids thought it was funny." Why did Mason think someone was out to get her?

"I'm not going to let anyone get to you."

"How did we get from vandalism to someone trying to get

me?" She placed her hands on his upper arms. "Mason, let's just call the police and put in a report. Then maybe have it towed to J.D.'s. I'll press charges if it was a deliberate, malicious act, but I want to get to the bottom of this first." It had to have been some prank, right? Amelia was trying to convince herself that it was nothing, but a small pit began to form in her gut.

"Fine," Mason said, turning his back to them and crossing his arms over his chest.

"I'll call the police," Rosie said, as she hurried to the back room.

Amelia could feel just how agitated Mason was. Anger was radiating out of him like a wave. She reached out and touched his shoulder. "Hey, it's okay. Nothing happened." She glanced down at Cassie, who was clutching at her hip. "Cassie's fine. Right, sweetheart?"

Cassie nodded. "Daddy won't let anything happen to us."

"See?" She squeezed his shoulder. "Everything will be okay."

He relaxed and turned back to them. His face was still tense, but his eyes had returned to normal. "It will be," he said. "I'll make sure."

The police arrived fifteen minutes later. Mason took the officer to the back to show him the car. Minutes later, they came back and the officer began to take their statement.

"Was there anything else unusual?" Officer Benton asked Amelia as he wrote in a notepad.

"I really didn't see much, just that the car was trashed."

"Do you suspect anyone who could do this? An enemy? Ex-boyfriend?"

Amelia could feel Mason tense beside her. "No," she said. "I just moved back to Blackstone a couple weeks ago."

"You're Ben Walker's sister, right, Miss Walker? And you're related to the Lennoxes?"

"Yes. But what does that—" She stopped. "You think this might be from that anti-shifter group?"

"Anti-shifter group?" Mason asked, his voice rising. "What are you talking about?"

Officer Benton frowned at Mason. "You're new here too, right?" Mason nodded and Benton continued. "A few weeks back, there was an attack on Blackstone. A major anti-shifter organization tried to blow up the entire town."

"Blow up the town?"

"Yeah. It was bad. I'm sure Miss Walker can fill you in. Normally, I would put this down to some kind of prank, but since then, we've been on high alert," Benton explained. "We'll dig deeper, see if there's any connection." He closed his notepad.

"You'll keep us updated?" Mason asked.

"Even if it is just a prank?" Amelia added, giving Mason the side-eye.

"Will do. And of course, we'll call you in if we bring in any suspects."

Officer Benton wrapped things up, and then left. The whole ordeal took about an hour, and Amelia was glad it was over. At least for now. Mason looked like he was not going to let this go.

"J.D. said she'll take care of it." Mason slipped his phone back into his jacket pocket. "She'll let us know what time we can come by tomorrow and see what can be done."

"Thanks for taking care of that." She felt a headache coming on. "I should get home. I still have work tomorrow. I can call Kate or Sybil—"

"I'm taking you home," Mason declared.

She was too drained to protest. "Fine."

Mason's hands gripped the wheel so tight, his knuckles turned white. He drove slowly and carefully, nodding as Amelia gave him directions, but hardly saying a word. When they stopped outside her house, he turned to her.

"I changed my mind. You shouldn't be here alone. I'll call your brother and—"

"Hold on!" she hissed. "Mason, have you gone insane?" She looked behind her in the back seat. Cassie was fast asleep in her car seat. "Let's talk outside." She yanked the door open and slipped outside. By the time she shut the door, Mason was already in front of her. She glared at him, her hands on her hips. "Now, tell me why you're overreacting?"

"Overreacting? Someone wants to hurt you."

She rolled her eyes. "You don't know that. Did you see any evidence? A note or a threat?"

He gritted his teeth. "I just know it. I can feel it. This was directed at you, Amelia. What was Benton talking about? The anti-shifters?"

Amelia sighed. "It's a very long story, but turns out, there was a big, underground anti-shifter organization that planned to destroy Blackstone. They kidnapped Luke's stepson and mate, too. But that's all done now. Their leader's in jail and as far as we know, the organization's leadership is in the wind."

Mason's lips thinned. "But there could be more of them out there?"

"Yes, but …" Kate and Sybil had told her about the Shifter Protection Agency operating in Blackstone but she wasn't sure if she should tell Mason. It was supposed to be a secret that they were working right under everyone's noses, hidden on the fifteenth floor of the Lennox Corp. building. But then again, it might reassure Mason that Blackstone was safe for him and Cassie. The thought of them leaving …. "Mason, let's not jump to conclusions. Besides, Cassie is fine and—"

"I'm not talking about Cassie," he growled. He leaned forward and she realized how close he was. His scent tickled her nose and the warmth of his body shot desire straight to her core. "I need … to keep you safe."

"Mason." She tilted her head up and she wasn't sure if she had moved forward or if Mason had bent his head down, but she suddenly felt his lips on hers.

Strong arms wound around her, pulling her to a hard chest. His mouth was gentle and sweet, with a hint of desperation that made her ache. Because she felt it too; that longing that seemed to have been inside her for years. She moved her mouth against his, unable to stop herself from opening her lips so he could dip his tongue into her mouth.

She knew she should have pushed him away, but instead, she moved her hands up his chest and around his neck, digging her fingers into his nape to bring him closer. He groaned, then pressed her up against the truck, his body covering hers.

He tasted the same—hot, masculine, and all Mason. She realized how much she missed this, being in his arms, kissing him and that ache inside her was still there, even after all these years. Which was why she pushed him away.

"Mason." Her voice sounded much breathier than she intended. "We can't—"

Mason silenced her with his mouth, urgent and wanting. He kissed her hard, his teeth grazing at her lips, leaving her feeling branded when he pulled away. "Don't say we can't."

Amelia felt her throat tighten. "Mason, this is crazy. We're not going down this road again." She dropped her gaze to her shoes.

"Why not? Do you really feel nothing for me?" He shook her gently, urging her to look at him.

And she did—gaze into the depths of his light blue eyes. Her mouth went dry, unable to speak.

"My feelings haven't changed," he confessed. "And I want you back."

His words made her heart ache. "Mason, please. Don't say things you don't mean."

"I do mean them." He leaned down to kiss her again, but she put a hand on his chest to stop him. "What do I have to do to show you?"

"I …" She was at a loss for words. On one hand, her brain was screaming at her to get away so he couldn't hurt her again. How could this work, anyway? He had Cassie, who needed him. Once again, there was no way she could get between him and his kid.

But on the other hand, something else deep inside was telling her to take the plunge.

"I don't know, Mason." She bit her lip.

"But that's not a no," he declared.

She looked up at him wryly, a smile tugging at her lips. "That's how you're interpreting this?"

He gave her a grin. "I'll take whatever I can get." He leaned down, nuzzled her neck, and brushed his lips against her ear making her shiver. "As long as you don't say no, I won't back away."

She sighed and leaned back against the truck. "I still don't know if I can do this."

"I'll do whatever it takes." There was a promise in his

words that was unspoken, and that made her shiver again. "I'll be patient. I can wait forever."

God, he was being so sweet and sincere, she didn't think she could resist him. She turned her head toward the back seat of the truck. "Cassie," she said. The girl was still fast asleep, as far as she could tell. "You need to take her home and get her to bed."

Mason braced his hands on the truck and pushed himself off her. "You have my number," he said. "Call me for anything. And have your phone next to you."

"I don't—" She stopped when she saw the serious look on his face. "Fine." She turned away from him, but a hand on her arm made her stop. "Mason."

He pulled her to him again, and she didn't have time to protest. Her body pressed against his and his lips landed on hers, and just like that, she lost all thought. It was familiar and wonderful, and sensations she couldn't put a name to ran through her body.

"I'll take you to work tomorrow," he said when he pulled away. "Go inside and lock your door."

"Uh … okay." Her knees wobbled slightly as she turned away, and it was a miracle she managed to get all the way to her front door without collapsing. Her hands shook as she put her key in the door. As soon as she got inside, she braced herself against the closed door. When she heard the truck pull away, she let out the breath she didn't realize she'd been holding.

Amelia touched her lips. They felt swollen and branded by that kiss. She still couldn't believe he did that. Or that he said he wanted her back. But, did she want him back? Could she risk her heart again? And what about Cassie? She needed Mason right now, and Mason didn't need to divide his attention between her and his daughter. Just like before, there was no question that Cassie came first.

She let out another long sigh and straightened her shoulders. Her mind was confused, and all she needed was rest. Between her car being vandalized and Mason's kiss, she couldn't think. She needed to pull herself together before Mason came back in the morning.

CHAPTER TWELVE

Mason got up bright and early the next day and got Cassie ready for day care. He got her showered, dressed, and fed, then loaded her up in the car. As soon as he dropped her off, he headed straight to Amelia's house.

There was a resolve and determination in him that he hadn't felt before. He didn't sleep at all, but he wasn't tired or confused. He knew now more than ever that Amelia was his mate, and always would be. They were supposed to be together. His bear agreed wholeheartedly but urged him to hurry.

She's fine, he said to his bear. She had responded to his text message this morning as soon as she was awake. He stayed up, waiting by his phone in case Amelia called. If he didn't have Cassie at home, he would have staked out her house. But, he knew Amelia was fine. For now.

Last night, he had been in a rage. Seeing her car trashed like that sent his instincts flaring. *Danger,* his bear had said. Their mate was in danger. His bear had never steered him wrong. Someone wanted to hurt Amelia. But who? He walked around the car, but couldn't trace any animal scents, so he knew it wasn't a shifter. Plus, the tires had been slashed and the body scratched by a small pen knife, not claws. All signs pointed to a human culprit. Did someone from the anti-shifter organization target Amelia because she was related to the Lennoxes? Or did they know she was vulnerable because she wouldn't be able to shift and defend herself? He had to find out more about this group. Maybe call up some old navy buddies.

He filed that away in his mental to-do list as soon as he pulled up in front of Amelia's house. His senses and instinct told him that everything was fine, and that she was safe inside.

He got out of the car and walked to her front door. His finger had barely touched the doorbell when the door opened.

"Mason," she greeted. "Good morning."

He braced a hand on the doorjamb. "It certainly is." She looked gorgeous this morning, as she always did. But there was something about her this morning ... he couldn't put his finger on it. She wore her usual office attire of a suit jacket and skirt, but she had put on some makeup and left her hair down. A blush crept onto her cheeks, and he couldn't help himself as he leaned down to kiss her. But, his lips landed on her cheek as she turned away.

"I ... I'm ready to leave if you are," she whispered, then ducked under his arm. "I don't want to be late."

"Right." Mason wasn't mad that she avoided his kiss. He promised her he'd be patient, and he meant it. He'd follow her around like a puppy, doing her bidding, if that's what it took. Because he was so damned in love with her, he would do anything to make her happy. "I'm ready."

He walked ahead of her, making sure he got to the truck

before she did so he could open the door and help her inside before getting into the driver's side.

The ride to her office was silent, but not uncomfortable. Mason glanced over at Amelia every few seconds, just to make sure she was okay. She was looking out the window, a wistful look on her face. Though he wanted to know what was on her mind, he didn't want to break the comfortable silence between them. Soon, they arrived outside her building.

She put a hand on his arm as he reached for his door. "You don't have to open the door for me."

"I know, but I should."

She gave him a weak smile. "I can do it. I don't want you to be late to work. I know you're supposed to start early."

"It's fine, I called in and said I'd be late." He remembered the message he got this morning. "Oh. J.D. told me she wanted to see you today and go over the damage. Around three o'clock?"

Amelia grimaced. "Ugh. I almost forgot. I'll ask Erin if I can pop out. She knows what happened, and she says to do whatever needs to be done."

He touched her cheek. "It'll be fine. Why don't I pick you up and we can go together?"

"Don't be silly," she said. "I don't need you to hold my hand."

He shrugged. "I need to be there anyway, I got some business to take care of." He could use the sale of the Harley as an excuse.

"Oh. Okay then. But you don't need to drive all the way here, and then double back to J.D.'s. It's not practical. I'll call a cab service and meet you there."

He wasn't sure he liked that plan, but Amelia seemed skittish all of a sudden and he didn't want to make her feel suffocated. "All right then," he said. "I'll see you there at three? Then we can swing by and get Cassie afterward. I still owe you that dinner."

She rolled her eyes but laughed. "How can I forget?"

Mason got out of work a little early and arrived at J.D.'s in no time. The garage was busy today, and there was no empty spot inside, so he parked the truck around the corner. Amelia said she was already on her way and waiting for her cab, so he decided to hang around. The place brought back good memories of working with Tim in his garage.

"Hey, Grimes!" J.D. called when he walked into the garage. The mechanic wasn't dressed in coveralls like the last time, but rather, in jeans, heels, and a red tank top which showed off a sleeve tattoo covering one arm. Her blonde hair was tied back in a ponytail, and her face was clean of dirt and grease.

"Hey J.D.," he greeted. "Busy today, yeah?"

"Tell me about it. My guys have been complaining the whole morning." She rolled her eyes. "I also gotta go and meet up with a supplier." She nodded to her generous cleavage spilling out of her tank top. "These babies get me a discount all the time, so I take out the big guns when I can."

"Err." He politely looked away from her breasts. "Well, thanks for taking care of Amelia's car."

"For her? No prob at all. I went to school with Amelia and she was nice to me. Not like those other stuck-up bitches who only saw me as a lowly mechanic's daughter." She made a face, then shook her head. "I have to say, that car was trashed real good. It's a shame."

"Yeah, whatever you can do to help out would be great."

"Of course. Now," J.D. began, her tone changing, "there's something I'd like to discuss with you if you have a minute."

"What about?" Mason asked. "Is it about my Harley? Did you find a buyer?"

"No, still working on that, but I got a few bites. I have a proposition for you. I've been thinking it over, ever since you brought your ride here."

Mason was intrigued. "Okay?"

"I only do cars here, as you can see." J.D. glanced at her workshop. "But as the only mechanic in town, people come in to ask us to work on bikes. I can do a few small repairs, but for the big stuff, all I really do is patch 'em up and send them to the garage over in Verona Mills. But, with Blackstone booming, I've been getting more and more calls about bikes. So, I thought, why the fuck do I keep sending business away when I could be rolling in that dough, ya know?" She jerked a thumb toward a third warehouse on the east side of the compound. "I decided to expand and start doing bike repairs and custom work too. Unfortunately," she clucked her tongue, "the guy I hired to get things going flaked out on me. I already got everything done with the renovations and the equipment."

"Jeez. That sucks."

"Yeah, tell me about it." She let out an exasperated sigh. "I already sunk a couple thousand into it and everything's just sitting there as useful as tits on a nun. But, here's what I'm thinking: why don't you come and work for me?"

"What?" Mason wasn't sure he heard her right. "You want to give me a job?"

"Unless you already got one, of course."

"I do. But it's part-time, at the mines." The work wasn't hard, not for a shifter like him, but Mason knew it wasn't something he could do in the long term. Plus, he still needed to pay for all of those attorney's fees. "I didn't go to school or have any certification or anything," he pointed out.

"Neither do I," J.D. countered. "If you're not interested in the job—"

"I am," he said quickly, before she changed her mind.

"I don't have any work for you right now, but I had a couple of people interested when I told them I was starting this. I'll call them up and show them your work, then maybe I can bring you in when I have something for you. Once the business comes rolling in, we can talk about having you come in on a regular basis."

It wasn't a full-time job, but he'd take any stream of income he could. "Count me in then." He held out his hand.

"Fucking awesome." J.D. grasped his palm and gave it a strong squeeze. "Now, wanna come see my setup?"

"Fuck yeah."

J.D. led him to the workshop and showed him around. She really sprung for all the best tools and equipment, and Mason couldn't help but get excited. He could possibly get paid to do something he loved.

"This is great," he said, unable to keep excitement from his voice.

"Yeah, I'm glad I don't have to—fucking shit!" They were already headed out when J.D. suddenly slipped on the concrete. She landed awkwardly on her side with a soft thud. "Motherfucking bitch-tits!"

"Holy—" Mason bent down to help her, wrapping an arm around her waist to help her up. "Are you okay, J.D.?"

"Goddamn heels! I'm never wearing these again!" She cursed, and then kicked off her shoes. "Shit! Fuck, fuck, fucking fuck! It hurts!"

"Jesus, sorry." He held her up so she could get the weight off her foot. "Is it broken?"

She looked down. "Nah. Just a sprain probably. And it'll heal quick."

This close to her, Mason could smell the scent of fur. Something feline, for sure, but his nose wasn't sensitive enough to tell what kind. "Let's go to your office and get some ice for the pain."

Mason slipped his arm around her, keeping her propped up as she hobbled along. Hoots and hollers greeted them as they exited. With his arms around J.D. and her body pressed up against his, Mason realized it must have looked like they were locked in an embrace.

"Get your minds out of the gutter and get back to work," she shouted, then looked at Mason apologetically. "Sorry, sometimes I think I work with children. I—Oh, Amelia! You're here."

Mason looked ahead, following J.D.'s gaze. Amelia was standing outside the office, arms crossed over her chest, and expression stony. Her nostrils flared as they drew closer, and Mason swore he saw a flash of anger in her eyes.

"Sorry, I'm late," she said, her voice tight. "But I see you guys are busy anyway. So, I'll see myself out." She turned on her heel and walked toward the gate.

"Busy?"

J.D. looked confused, but Mason knew what was going on. He cursed inwardly. "Are you okay? Can you make it on your own?"

She glanced at Amelia's retreating back then back at Mason. "Shit." She disentangled herself from him. "I can make it to my office. I can feel it healing already, but damn it, sorry I got you in trouble with your old lady."

"Old lady?" He chuckled. "Don't worry, it's not anything that can't be fixed. I'll see you later, J.D." He waved goodbye, and then hurried off, following Amelia's trail. As he exited the compound and glanced around. He spied a flash of blonde hair, and saw her turn the corner.

He quickly caught up with her and grabbed her arm. "Hey," he said. "Where are you going?"

Slowly, she turned around. Her face was a frosty mask. "Home. And don't touch me." She tried to yank her arm away, but his grip was firm.

"What's the matter?" He knew the answer of course but wanted to hear it from her.

"Nothing."

"Nothing?" He raised a brow at her. "Are you jealous?"

"Jealous? Ha! Why would I be jealous? Just because she was rubbing her breasts on you?" She huffed. "Besides, you didn't seem to mind.

"Amelia," he began. "It's not what you think. J.D. was showing me her new bike workshop. She wants me to work there. But, she slipped and sprained her ankle, and I was helping her." She looked away, but he tipped her chin to look at him. "I would never look at another woman. I've never been with anyone else since you."

"No one?" Her lips pursed and her eyes narrowed. "No other girl? Not even your ex-wife?"

"No way." The memory of disgust he had felt when Jenna threw herself at him when he was home was coming back and made him want to throw up. "Not that I didn't try with anyone else." He wasn't going to lie to her. He had been single for a year and attempted some one-night stands and pickups. "But I just couldn't."

"Why not?"

"Because they weren't you. None of them were you."

A breath escaped her lips. "Mason …" Her voice broke. "I haven't … either."

Mason felt relief, but he wouldn't have blamed her if she'd been with other men. He pulled her to him, planting his mouth on top of hers. Fuck, he'd been waiting for this all day, to feel her lips on his, and it was even better than he'd imagined.

Amelia's arms wound around his neck. She pushed her body at him desperately, and the scent of her need filled his nose. He moved his hands up to cup her breasts, squeezing and feeling the weight of them in his hands. His dick went hard as steel and when he brushed his erection against her hip, she opened her mouth and gasped.

"Mason," she whispered. "What time do you have to pick up Cassie?"

The desire clouding his mind cleared for a moment. "In about an hour. Why?"

She tugged at his hand. "My place is closer."

He didn't need a second invitation. "My truck's just over there."

CHAPTER THIRTEEN

Amelia's heart was running a mile a minute as Mason drove them to her house. *This was really happening.* But at this point it felt inevitable, and she was tired of denying that she wanted him. And seeing him today with J.D., well, that pushed her over the edge. She didn't know what to make of his confession, but she put it out of her mind because it scared the bejesus out of her.

It was a quick ride, and he practically dragged her out of the truck and to the front door. She somehow dug her keys out of her purse and let them in. When the door closed behind them, she found herself slammed up against it, Mason's body trapping hers.

"Oh!" She shivered when his mouth found her neck, and she leaned her head back to give him better access. He knew how much she loved having her neck kissed and drove her crazy.

She was taking off her suit jacket and his hands were fumbling with her blouse. He grew impatient and just grabbed her collar, ripping the fabric down the middle and sending buttons flying everywhere. He yanked her bra cups down, exposing her nipples to the cool air, making them pucker. He bent his head down and sucked in a nipple.

"Mason!" She cried out and raked her fingers into his scalp.

His hand snuck up under her skirt, pushing it up over her thighs, and his fingers hooked into the waistband of her panties and tugged them down. She knew she was already wet and his fingers slipped into her easily. Between his mouth and fingers, she was lost in the sensation. The moment his thumb found her clit, her body shuddered and her pussy drenched his fingers with wetness as she came.

"Fuck," Mason cursed as he popped a nipple out of his mouth. "Up ... stairs ... bedroom." She managed to shuck off her panties from around her knees and what remained of her blouse, while Mason took his shirt off and unzipped his jeans. She sucked in a breath, watching the muscles on his chest and arms ripple. God, he was the sexiest man she'd ever been with, and her eyes devoured the taut tanned skin, the perfectly-formed pecs, and that set of six-pack abs she loved to lick and bite. He shoved his jeans and underwear down, and his erect cock jutted out.

"Amelia."

She looked up at him and saw the desire in his eyes, and she felt consumed just by his gaze. Mason made a grab for her and dragged her toward the stairs. Halfway up, she pushed him against the wall and held his jaw in her hands, then kissed him. Their lips and tongues clashed in an urgent dance.

"I can't wait, darlin'," he said when he broke the kiss. "I need to be inside you."

Mason pulled her down, so they were on their knees. She

couldn't wait either, her body needing him. He pushed her back, making her lie back as he spread her legs.

"Now," she said.

He leaned over her, got between her legs, and gathered her to him. She felt the blunt tip of his cock at her entrance, plunging into her slowly. She gasped, her body slowly adjusting to his size and girth, and she relaxed when he was fully inside her.

He tugged her head back, and then devoured her mouth in another kiss. As his tongue danced with hers, he began to move. Short, shallow strokes at first, but when he started to go deeper, she angled her hips, wanting more of him inside her.

Mason grunted and pulled up her legs by locking his arms under her knees. She got what she wanted—and he was buried inside her deep, hitting all the right spots as he continued to thrust into her.

"Mason!" She looked up and he was staring down at her, his light blue eyes concentrated on her. He leaned down to give her another deep kiss, all the while fucking harder and harder into her.

His mouth muffled her scream as the pleasure overwhelmed her. But before she could come down, Mason quickly lifted her up, their bodies never disconnecting. She thought he would carry her to the bedroom, but instead, he flipped them over so he was laying back on the steps and she was on top.

Those blue eyes stared up at her, and she lost herself in them for a moment. As he reached up to cup her breasts, she began to move.

"Oh!" She used her knees for leverage, lifting her hips up, and then plunging down. That made Mason groan and pinch her nipples, which just made her move faster. She grabbed the bannister, using it to steady herself as she rode him. God, she loved the feeling of him inside her like this, thick and long and hitting all the right spots.

Mason was thrusting his hips up at her, getting deeper inside her. He sat up, shifting his hips so she straddled him completely. She rode him harder, bringing herself down on him completely as he continued to move in time to meet her thrusts.

"Mason!" His fingers moved between them, strumming her clit until her back arched. "Oh God! I'm coming!" That only urged him on, and he moved faster, his hips bucking into her and his thumb and forefinger pinching her hardened nub. Oh fuck, she was coming, her body shaking hard and her vision turning white behind her eyelids.

Mason let out a long grunt and pushed into her one last time before she felt his cock twitch and pump his seed into her. Warmth flooded her, and as she slowed down, Mason pulled her to him, his lips ravaging her in a hard kiss. He pulled her back down, taking her with him, and she lay on top of his chest, listening to the sound of his heartbeat as it slowed to normal.

Amelia should have been exhausted, but she felt wide awake and alive. Her body was sore, but something inside her was singing out, like it had been trapped for a long time. The whole thing felt like a tidal wave—inevitable and unstoppable, and she had no choice but to let it carry her away.

Mason's hand lazily stroked her back, and she looked up at him. He stared down at her, his expression content and his gaze half-lidded.

She sucked in a breath. "Do you have to go soon?"

"We have time."

She let out a whoop as Mason stood up in one motion, placing her over his shoulder so she was upside down. "Mason!" She laughed, and then let out a shriek when he spanked her ass playfully. "Put me down."

"Not yet." He lumbered up to the second floor and walked down the hallway to her bedroom. When he reached her bed, he plopped her down on the mattress, eliciting another shriek from her. He joined her, his weight and size making the mattress dip.

"I—" She gasped when he pulled her knees toward him, spreading her thighs. He was hard again, and he wrapped a fist around his shaft, then directed it at her aching core.

He filled her in one stroke and she wrapped her legs around him to take him as deep as she could. Mason made love to her, slow and deliberate, with such aching fierceness that she felt the tears gathering at the corner of her eyes. When he saw them, he leaned down and licked them away.

"Mason!" she cried out when she felt her orgasm building. He moved faster, deeper, his arms winding around her to pull her close. He held her like that as she rode out her orgasm, his lips claiming hers again in a tender kiss. She sighed when her body relaxed. Now, she felt like she could sleep for a hundred years and closed her eyes.

Mason didn't move, keeping her pinned underneath him. He propped himself up on his elbow, looking down at her and stroking her cheek.

"Amelia," he rasped. "I love you. I never stopped loving you."

Her eyes flew open and her gaze clashed with his. She opened her mouth but nothing came out.

"It's okay. You don't have to say it back." But she had seen his expression falter for a second.

"It's not that I …" Oh God, her chest felt like it was going to implode. Her mind whirled with confusion and she pushed at him, then rolled away. "Mason, I just can't … It's not that I don't want … I don't know if I *can*." The lump stuck in her throat made her sob.

"Shh …" A gentle hand touched her shoulder.

She turned around to face him. His expression was so sincere and she wanted desperately to say the words back. "Mason."

"It's okay, Amelia." He pulled her to him and kissed her forehead. "I'll love enough for the both of us."

Amelia didn't say anything, and just tucked her face against his chest. She hoped that would be enough for now.

Amelia dozed off for a few minutes, but Mason rolling out of bed woke her. "Do you have to go pick up Cassie?"

"We have to go pick her up," he said, as he reached for her.

She moved away. "We?"

"I told her you'd be there." He stood there, fully naked, hands on his hips.

Amelia wanted to throw a pillow at his stupid, handsome face. "What exactly did you tell her?"

"I said that if she finished her breakfast this morning, the three of us would go out for tacos." He grinned at her. "You can't disappoint a little girl, now, can you?"

This time, she really did lob a pillow at him, which he easily knocked away. He growled, and then grabbed her ankles, making her shriek with indignation.

"C'mon, now, we don't want to be late."

"Fine," she grumbled as she got up from the bed. "But you're paying, and I'm having twenty tacos."

He laughed.

They quickly got dressed, and then headed to the day care. They were five minutes late, but Cassie was just so happy to see Amelia that she didn't complain at all.

"You came!" she said as she jumped into Amelia's arms.

"Of course." Amelia hugged the little girl tight, then turned a wry smile at Mason. "I heard you finished your breakfast this morning."

"I did!"

"Well, now it's time for tacos." She put Cassie down. "Your dad says I can have as much as I want."

Blackstone didn't have any Mexican restaurants, but Mason was happy to drive them all the way to Verona Mills to the same taco place they had dinner at. As promised, she ate twenty tacos, polishing each one off with a smile, much to Cassie's delight.

Mason drove them back, and soon Cassie was fast asleep again. He stopped the truck outside her house, got out, and walked over to her side to open the door.

"You don't have to keep doing that," she said wryly.

Mason took her hand and helped her down. "Yes, I do. Besides, Cassie needs to see what a real gentleman is like so she doesn't wind up with a loser when she grows up."

"I don't think that'll happen with you as her dad." Mason's arm quickly wrapped around her waist and pulled her close, then shut the door behind her. "Hmm ... I'm not sure a gentleman does this."

"I can't be a gentleman around you all the time." He leaned in and kissed her on the lips. Soft and innocent, but it sent her toes curling. "This isn't going to work."

"What?" She was still feeling dizzy, so she wasn't sure he heard him right.

"I'm not talking about *this*." He brushed his hip against her and she felt his bulge press up to her. "I mean, you, alone at home when whoever trashed your car is still out there, while I have to stay at home."

"Mason, are you still worried about that?" She pulled away from him. "Nothing has happened."

"Yet." She heard the snarl deep in his chest.

"You're being silly."

"I'm not taking chances with your safety." His expression was serious. "I stayed up all night, waiting for you to call."

"Well, what do you want to do about it?" she challenged.

"Pack a bag and stay with us."

"What? I can't do that."

"I know our place is small and not as nice as yours—"

"Mason," she said in an exasperated voice. "It's not about that. But, it's not exactly appropriate, having me stay in your bed with your daughter a few feet away."

"I can sleep on the floor," he offered.

"Now you're being ridiculous." She threw her hands up. "You don't have to divide your time between me and Cassie, you know. Why don't you just stay at my place? I've got an extra bedroom and—" She stopped short, realizing what she had said. But, she didn't take it back. Somehow, it just felt right, having Cassie and Mason with her.

"Well, if you're offering …" He gave her another devastatingly handsome smile.

"We'll say it's a sleepover." Of course, that also meant Cassie would have her own room down that hall. "Or just, maybe tell her that you're having a gas leak or something and that's why you're staying over?"

Mason didn't answer her because he was already opening the door and pushing her back inside. When he slipped into the driver's seat, he turned back to Cassie and nudged her awake. "Guess what, baby? We're going to have a sleepover at Amelia's. Let's head back and pack your pajamas."

Cassie jolted awake and cried, "Yay!"

Amelia shook her head and slapped a palm on her forehead. Still, she'd be lying if she said she wasn't happy that she'd be around Cassie and Mason more.

CHAPTER FOURTEEN

AMELIA HUMMED HAPPILY to herself as she worked on the plans for a new client. This particular building offered new office spaces in the ever-expanding South Blackstone.

"That looks phenomenal," Erin said as she came up from behind. "Keysmart Properties will be ecstatic."

"I finished the interiors too," Amelia said proudly. "Did you see them?"

"I did. Girl, you're on a tear! What's got all your creative juices flowing these days?"

Amelia couldn't help but blush. "I've just been really inspired lately."

It had been two days since Mason and Cassie came over for a "sleepover" and they had yet to leave. Having them in her house just felt so right, she didn't know why. Cassie didn't question the hows and whys, but she seemed happy enough in Amelia's guest bedroom. And as for Mason …

She gave an involuntary shiver and blushed again. Being with him was just indescribable. It wasn't just the sex—which was even better than she remembered—but she hadn't felt so content in ... well, ever. Sleeping next to him and waking up next to him was the best feeling ever.

Amelia chewed on her lip. Mason hadn't said "I love you" again since that first time. Somehow, it annoyed the heck out of her. *You're being silly*, she told herself. She hadn't said it back either. Maybe he was just giving her space.

But, did she love him? It's like the words were there, stuck in her vocal chords, but she couldn't form them out loud. She didn't want to confront her feelings, as she was afraid that this was all a dream and she could lose it all when she woke up. Just like when the bond had broken the first time.

A loud vibration from her purse made her turn her head, and she reached inside to grab her phone. *Mason.* "Hey, what's up?"

"Amelia." His voice was gravelly.

"What's wrong?" She could hear the worry in his voice.

"There's been a small accident at the mines."

"What?" She stood up from her chair. "Are you okay? Is it Ben?"

"No, no, darlin', it's not bad. One of the guys had a mishap." Mason sighed. "But, it's bad enough that Ben had to go with him to Blackstone Hospital."

"Oh, thank God."

"But, Ben asked if I could stay behind and take care of a few things."

"Ah, I see." She paused. "Did you want me to pick up Cassie?"

"Do you mind?" he asked.

"Of course not. I'll swing by at five." Since Amelia's car was still under repair, she had been driving her dad's Jeep. "The day care should have an extra car seat I could borrow."

"Good." He sounded relieved.

"Why don't we get dinner and meet you at home? How does Chang Kee sound?" It had been their favorite Chinese takeout place, and she hadn't eaten there in ages.

"Sounds great. Make sure you get me a—"

"Double order of crab wontons and extra sauce," she finished.

"You remembered."

Amelia chuckled. "Of course I do. Now, go and take care of things. I'll see you at home."

"See you at home."

Home. Her rented house had never felt more like home than it did the last two days. And she knew it was all thanks to Mason and Cassie.

She turned back to her work and put some finishing touches on the plans. Before she knew it, it was already quarter to five. Amelia explained to Erin what happened, and her boss was only too happy to let her go early.

As she got out of the elevator and walked out into the street, a strange sensation crept up her spine. Her head snapped up, and then she glanced around. It was like someone was watching her. *Weird.* She was probably just feeling off.

Amelia drove straight to Lennox Corp. Mason had already called ahead and told Miss Irene that Amelia would be by to pick up Cassie. By the time she signed into the day care, Cassie and the borrowed car seat were waiting for her.

"'Melia!" Cassie immediately went in for a hug. "Guess what we did today?

She kissed the top of the girl's head. "What?"

"Well, first Miss Irene told us a story, and then …"

Amelia was happy to listen to Cassie babble and tell her about her day as they made their way back to the car and on the drive over to the Chinese place.

Chang Kee was located in a strip mall just outside of the main Blackstone town, but she didn't mind the drive as they had the best General Tso's chicken and chow mein she'd ever had. When the girl at the counter handed her their order, she paid and they headed out.

"Just walk behind me, okay, sweetie?" Amelia's hands were full as she had two bags in tow. "Oh, excuse me!" Distracted with trying to juggle the bags and Cassie, she nearly bumped into someone when she stepped out of the restaurant. She tried to sidestep, but the person—a woman—blocked her. "Do you mind?" Amelia said impatiently, looking behind her to check on Cassie.

"Actually, I do mind you fucking my ex-husband around my kid."

Amelia's blood froze in her veins and slowly, she turned her head forward. The woman in front of her had dark hair pulled back into a ponytail and wore a rumpled blouse and jeans. Most people would have called her pretty, but her scowling face was gaunt and the dark circles under her eyes marred her features. Upon closer inspection, Amelia recognized the chin and nose, which were so much like Cassie's. So, this was Jenna. Mason's ex-wife and Cassie's mom.

"Mommy?" Cassie peeked from behind Amelia.

"Cassie!" Jenna's expression changed and she bent down to reach for Cassie.

"Stay away from her!" Amelia growled, dropping the bags of food to the ground. She spread her arms, preventing her from getting too close.

"You bitch! You can't stop me from seeing my own kid!" Jenna hissed. "Cassie, come here now!" She reached for Cassie again, and Amelia knocked her hand away.

"You will not touch her!" Anger bubbled at the surface. "You're a fugitive from the law. I'm going to call the cops."

"Stop stalling, lady," a voice from behind said. "Get your kid *now*."

The voice sent a chill through her. Slowly, Amelia turned around. There were three men standing there, their gazes trained on Jenna. They didn't look like they were from around here. All three wore outfits that screamed big city—shiny leather shoes, sports jackets or polo shirts, and dark sunglasses.

One of them took off his glasses and shot Jenna a glare. "Well? Is this your kid? Grab her and let's go."

"No!" Amelia picked up Cassie and hugged her close, her hand on her head to keep her from turning. Cassie let out a cry. "Shh … it's okay sweetie, I'm here."

"That's what I'm trying to do, Tony!" Jenna protested, stamping her feet. "But this bitch won't give her to me."

"You'll get her over my dead body!" Amelia gritted her teeth.

Tony laughed. "Well, if that's what it takes," he turned to the two men behind him. Both guys opened their jackets and drew out their guns, pointing them at Amelia and Cassie.

"No!" Jenna cried.

Amelia turned around to shield Cassie. "It's broad daylight! Are you really going to shoot me?" Despite her bravado, her heart was banging against her ribcage like a hammer.

"Fine," Tony spat. "Take them both then!"

Before Amelia could run, she felt the press of a metal barrel on her back. "After I shoot you, I'll shoot the kid," a voice whispered in her ear. "Now, come with us."

Her knees and her arms felt weak. She couldn't let them hurt Cassie. Dammit. She felt the tears of despair building in her throat. If she had her bear, she could tear these guys to shreds. She would even survive a couple of bullets. But no, Cassie's safety was more important. A fierce, protective instinct rose up in her. "Fine," she said. "But if you hurt her, I swear to God—"

"You'll what, girly?" The barrel pushed harder into her spine. "Now, go."

Amelia kept her grip on Cassie tight as she followed the three men and Jenna to the parking lot of the strip mall. She kept soothing Cassie, running a hand up and down her back as they walked. When they got to a dark-colored van, the door slid open.

"Get in."

Amelia scooted inside, keeping Cassie on her lap. The girl was sobbing softly now, and Amelia could feel her tears as it soaked her blouse. *I won't let anything happen to you,* she vowed.

There was another man sitting there wearing dirty sweats, who moved to make room. Tony sat in the seat across her, Jenna beside him, and then the man with the gun beside Amelia.

"I don't know what the hell is going on," Amelia began. "But you can't get away with kidnapping us!"

"If you'd mind your own business, you wouldn't even be here," Tony shot back. "We just want the kid because that's the only way this broad," he jabbed Jenna with his elbow, "and her boyfriend," he pointed his chin at the man beside Amelia, "would tell us where they stashed my cash."

"Cash?" Amelia said. "I have money. If we stop by the ATM, you can have all of it. Just let Cassie go."

Tony laughed. "Really now? You got six-and-a-half G's in your bank account we can take out now?"

Jesus. Over half a million? What kind of convenience store did Jenna and her boyfriend rob?

"This is your fault," the man beside Amelia said to Jenna. "I told you we don't need her." He sneered at Cassie. "We should have taken the cash and ran."

"Allowing you to convince me to leave her was the biggest mistake I ever made," Jenna screamed. "And the second biggest was getting together with your stupid ass, Doug!"

"How was I supposed to know that last store we hit was a front for the freakin' *mob*." Doug looked meaningfully at Tony.

"Maybe the bags of cash you stole in the secret storage room in the back should've tipped ya off?" Tony said dryly.

"We shoulda hightailed it to the border," Doug sulked. "But no, you wanted your kid. And then you saw her," he sneered at Amelia, "all over your stupid ex and you lost it. Why did you have to trash her car?"

"Because she's a whore who deserved it." Jenna shot daggers at Amelia with her eyes.

"We shoulda just grabbed the brat, like we planned," Doug said. "Then *they* wouldn't have caught up with us."

"We would have anyway. Do you think I would let some two-bit criminals like you just run away?" Tony turned to Amelia and Cassie. "But, now that we've got your kid, tell us where you hid the cash."

"You promise not to hurt her?" Jenna asked.

Tony smiled like a shark, with all his white teeth showing. "Of course."

"Shut up! Don't you say anything, you bitch!" Doug screamed.

"Go to hell, Doug!" Jenna tried to claw at Doug but Tony pulled her back. "You—"

Something bumped into the van, making it veer off the road. The driver was able to take control of the van, but the passengers inside shoved and jostled against each other. The engine roared and the van sped up.

"What the fuck is going on?" Tony asked.

"Someone's after us," the driver shouted back.

"Cops?"

"No! Some guy in a truck. But don't worry, boss, I'll lose him."

"You better!" Tony turned back to Jenna. "Now, where is the cash?"

Jenna's lower lip trembled. "It's—"

"You whore!" Doug screamed.

It all happened in a blur. One minute, Doug was screaming his head off, then the guy next to Amelia pulled his gun. The van swerved again, and somehow, Doug reached over and grabbed the guy's gun.

"This is your fault," he shouted and pointed the gun at Cassie's head.

Jenna screamed, and then something hit the van, sending everyone flying off their seats. Amelia held onto Cassie, trying to shield her from whatever was coming. *Please.* She didn't know to whom she was pleading to. *Please keep her safe.*

Heat spread through her body, and at first, she thought she'd been stabbed or shot. But there wasn't any pain. Only something warm. And familiar.

Amelia let out an inhuman roar. As she stretched her arms to grab the gun in Doug's hand, her limbs became longer, the pops of bone breaking and stretching echoing in the small space. Dark blonde fur sprouted out of her skin and she felt her teeth growing.

"What the fuck!" Tony shouted. "She's one of *them*!"

Amelia's body had grown so big, she pushed everyone out of the way. The van suddenly stopped, and by the time she was fully transformed into her monster grizzly, her giant block head had torn through the roof of the van. She crouched down, her arms wrapped around Cassie, who had clung to her fur tightly.

Stay with me, she said from inside her bear. *I'll keep you safe, little cub.*

"Get me the fuck outta here!" Tony cried.

The van door swung open and everyone, except Doug, flew out. Doug was trapped between the door and Amelia. He was screaming his head off, and Amelia's bear was so annoyed it slapped a massive paw over the man's head. It must have been too forceful as he was knocked out cold.

The grizzly roared, and Cassie tightened her grip. *That's it,* Amelia thought. *Don't let go, Cassie. You're safe with me.*

There was more shouting outside, and the grizzly forced its way out of the wrecked van, the metal screeching loudly as its claws tore through it like tissue paper. It kept one arm around Cassie, keeping her covered as it lumbered out.

"Shoot it! Shoot it!"

The grizzly turned its head. Two of the men who had escaped the van were now pointing their guns at the bear.

No!

The bear roared in anger, but it kept Cassie shielded. Inside her bear, Amelia braced for the pain of the bullets, but when the shots rang out, they missed completely.

A large, white blur whizzed by, charging at the two men. Amelia cried out and her bear growled.

Mine!

Mason's polar bear knocked the two men aside, his black claws slashing at them. The grizzly wanted to join in, to kill the men who tried to hurt Cassie, but Amelia reined her in. *Keep Cassie safe*, she reminded it. *Let our mate get revenge.*

There were screams and gurgles, then suddenly, silence. The polar bear trudged backwards, its pure white fur painted with red streaks. It locked eyes with the grizzly, and suddenly, Amelia found herself staring at Mason, inside his polar bear, looking back at her.

"What the fuck is going on?" Tony screamed. He and Jenna were on the ground, their eyes wide with fear and bodies frozen in shock. When the sounds of police sirens rang through the air, Tony scrambled to get up. "I'm getting the hell out of here."

The grizzly growled, and the polar bear charged forward, getting up on its hind legs. Tony suddenly stopped and dropped to the ground. "All right! All right!" He held up his hands, and then sank down to the ground.

The two bears flanked Tony and Jenna, preventing them from escaping. Cassie clung to the grizzly the whole time, her face buried in its soft fur. The cops arrived minutes later, their sirens blaring as they stopped by the side of the road.

"Jesus, what is going on?" Officer Benton said as he surveyed the scene. He looked at the two bears. "Mr. Grimes? Miss Walker?" He looked back and called one of the other officers. "Jones! Grab the blankets in the cruiser and help out those two."

As soon as the officer offered her the blanket, Amelia tucked her bear deep inside her, her body shrinking down to its normal size in no time. Her normal human arms wrapped around Cassie before the girl slipped down, and they both sank to the ground. A rough blanket dropped over her.

"I'm here, Cassie," she soothed. "It's me. I'm here."

Cassie looked up at her, her cheeks stained with tears. "I know, 'Melia. That's why I wasn't scared. You and your bear protected me."

She held Cassie tight. "I—"

"Cassie! Amelia!"

She looked up. Mason had turned back to his human form too, and he shrugged off the offer of a blanket from the officer. Instead, he ran to them then scooped them both up into his arms. "Oh, God, I thought I'd lost you." He rubbed his forehead against Cassie's, then looked straight at Amelia. "I was going to surprise you and show up at Chang Kee's. I was pulling in when I saw them take you." His teeth gnashed together. "I called the police and went after you."

Cassie scrambled into Mason's arms. "I was scared, Daddy. But 'Melia kept me safe."

"Oh, Mason." She hugged him back, his fresh mountain air scent like a soothing balm to her soul.

"Your bear … you have your bear back."

"I know." She didn't know how but … seeing Cassie in danger had brought her bear out. It wasn't gone; just hiding. It had been so hurt from the broken bond that it went into hibernation, deep inside her. But now, it was back, and Amelia felt whole for the first time in years. She took a deep breath, then glanced behind Mason. The police were hauling Tony, Jenna, and Doug away in handcuffs. "Mason, it was Jenna. She—"

"Shh." He put a finger on her lips. "We can talk about that later. There are more important things."

"Like what?"

Mason shifted Cassie to one arm, then used his free hand to pull her to him. "Like this." He leaned down and planted his mouth on hers. "I love you, Amelia."

"Mason, I love you too." She spoke the words freely, without hesitation. As they stood there, arms around each other, a familiar feeling wrapped around her. It was soothing and calm, like a gentle wave, but wrapped around them like a vortex. There was a roaring in her ears and when she looked up at Mason, the look on his face told her he felt it too.

"The bond." His voice broke. "I can feel it. It's back."

"Yes." She choked, tears streaming down her cheeks. "I never thought I would feel this way again. I love you, Mason."

"Daddy, what's happening?" Cassie asked, then turned to Amelia. "You love my daddy, 'Melia?"

Amelia smiled. "I do, Cassie. Your daddy is my mate."

Her mouth formed into a small *o*. "And you'll be with him forever? Like the dragon and the bear in your story?"

Mason shot her a confused look, but she just winked at him. "Yes, sweetie. I'll be with you both forever, if you'll have me."

Cassie wrapped her arms around her neck. "Thank you for being my daddy's mate. Now he won't be alone anymore. And yes, I want you to be with us."

Amelia's heart was filled with so much love, she thought it would burst out of her chest. She'd always thought that love was a finite thing, that having more people in your life meant that the love would always be divided until it grew smaller and smaller. But, she knew the truth now: love grew, the more you shared it. And, looking at Mason and Cassie, she knew there would be an abundance of love in her life from now on.

EPILOGUE

As was their custom, the Lennox-Walker clan gathered together for a barbecue on the last weekend of the summer. Once again, Hank and Riva Lennox, and James and Laura Walker, interrupted their retirement trip to come home. Of course, it wasn't a big bother to the two couples, especially for James and Laura, who had wanted to meet Mason and Cassie anyway. They planned to be in Blackstone for a week, and then be on their way once again, returning finally once Penny gave birth.

"And they—"

"Lived happily ever after!" Cassie finished.

James Walker grinned at her. "You know it!" He was sitting with Cassie and Grayson on the dock that stretched out over Blackstone Lake.

Instead of having the barbecue at the castle, the two families decided to have it at the lake. Hank and James had just finished building their lakeside cabins right before they left on their trip but didn't get the chance to bring everyone there together.

"Is Pawpaw telling you the story of Silas and Anastasia again?" Amelia asked as she approached the trio.

"Yeah! He tells it the best, just like you said, 'Melia," Cassie replied.

"I haven't heard it yet," Grayson added. "So, Cassie said I had to listen to it."

"What did you think?" James asked.

"Well," Grayson began thoughtfully, "I like that part where Silas dives in to rescue the dragon girl, but"—he made a face—"did it have to be a kissing story?"

James chuckled. "Ben pretty much said the same thing when he was your age." He ruffled the boy's hair. "But I have other stories too, you know. How 'bout I tell you the story of how Lucas Lennox and Eustace Walker outsmarted a whole pack of wolves?"

"Oh boy!" Grayson raised his fist. "What happened?"

"Maybe you guys can continue later," Amelia said. "Lunch is ready."

"Aww!" Both kids whined.

James hopped to his feet and offered the two toddlers a hand each. "C'mon, you munchkins. Stories later. Food now; I'm hungry." The two kids reluctantly stood up and grabbed onto him. He turned to Amelia. "Let's go."

The Lennox and Walker cabins stood side by side, with a privacy hedge in between, but they had a common backyard area. Picnic tables had been set up where the two properties met. The grill was set up on the Walker side, and Ben and Matthew were watching over the food. Hank, Riva, Laura, Penny, Sybil, and Tim were sitting on some patio chairs, chatting and drinking beers. Luke, Georgina, Christina, Catherine, Jason, Petros, and Kate were out swimming in the lake.

Amelia spotted Mason by himself, talking into his phone.

She walked over to him, and as soon as Mason locked eyes with her, a grin spread over his face.

"… All right, Gordon, I'll make sure I get those parts in by Monday." Mason nodded. "Yup. You have a good weekend too." He put the phone away and turned to Amelia.

A warm, familiar feeling settled over her, and when he slipped his arm around her to pull her close, her bear rumbled happily. She still couldn't believe it was back. It was like seeing an old friend again after a long time.

"Everything okay, mate?" Mason teased and she blushed. She let it slip one time that she loved it when he called her that and now he wouldn't stop.

"Yeah. You?"

"Yeah, all good. Just wanted to make sure I got everything right." Mason had only started working for J.D. two weeks ago, and already the clients were rolling in. In fact, he was booked for custom jobs for the next six months. He didn't even have to sell his Harley to pay for his legal bills anymore, as J.D. gave him a generous percentage of every build he did and brought him in as a partner.

She looked to Ben and Matthew, who waved them over. "Food will be ready in two minutes."

He kissed her temple. "Okay, let's go."

They walked over to the buffet table which was laden with all kinds of food. Soon, everyone had their plates piled high. Cassie cheered when Amelia finished four burgers and a whole rack of ribs, plus a helping of all the sides. Even Grayson was impressed.

When they were all done eating, everyone headed to the lake to go swimming. Amelia and Mason were happy to just sit on the dock, watching as Cassie held onto the polar bear swimming across the lake as she screamed, "Go, Uncle Tim, go!"

"Mason, Amelia," Laura called as she approached them. She was holding a wrapped box in her hand.

"Hey, Mom," Amelia said. "Aren't you going for a swim?"

"In a minute," she said. "But now that I have you guys alone, I wanted to give you this."

"You didn't have to," Mason said. "You've given us a lot of gifts." Indeed, when Laura and James first arrived, they came with a mountain of gifts, most of them for Cassie.

"This one is just for the two of you." Laura had a sparkle in her eye as she handed them the box. "Here. Open it."

Mason took the box and gingerly opened the intricate wrapping. He took out a small bowl and cupped it in his hands.

"It's beautiful," Amelia said, looking at the delicate pottery. It was a blue earthenware bowl with gold streaks all over the surface.

"What is it?" Mason asked.

"This bowl was made using a Japanese technique called *kinstugi* or 'golden repair'," Laura began. "See the veins? That's where the bowl was broken but was put back together using gold." She gave them a bright smile. "They say that the pieces repaired using this technique come out even more beautiful, because of the scars they bear. I thought you'd like it."

Amelia stared at the bowl, thinking about her mom's words. She looked at Mason, who was staring at her, his light blue eyes all lit up, and she knew he was thinking the same thing. This bowl was like their mating bond. It felt different; maybe a little worn and patched up, but just as beautiful as it had once been, and maybe even better.

"Thank you, Laura," Mason said, finally breaking the hushed silence. "It's gorgeous."

Laura stood up and dusted her hands on her thighs. "We'll take care of Cassie for now. Why don't you guys go and enjoy some quiet time together?" She winked at Mason.

Amelia narrowed her eyes suspiciously at the two of them, but before she could say anything, Mason stood up, grabbed her hand, and pulled her up. "Let's go for a walk."

She let him lead her back into the woods, content to just walk behind him. They walked out for a good twenty minutes, until they came to a small clearing. Amelia breathed in the clean air and wrapped her arms around him from behind. He turned around and kissed her forehead.

She looked up and noticed the frown on his face. "Everything okay?"

"Yeah." But she could feel the tension in his body. "I'm just, you know, worried about Cassie."

Amelia leaned her head on his shoulder. She knew what he'd been thinking about. Yesterday, Moynahan gave them some news: Jenna was being held in prison and it wasn't looking good. The cases against her and Doug were solid, not to mention, because of their involvement with the mob, the case was now a federal one. There was a chance she could be put away for at least twenty years.

"I don't know what to say to Cassie." He hugged her tighter. "About everything. I don't want to hide anything from her; she'll figure out she's different, eventually. But I don't want to hurt her either."

"You'll work it out," she said. "Just be honest with her. Kids are resilient, you know? And Cassie is an amazing girl."

His lips curled up at the corners. "She is."

"And whatever happens, I'll be here for you both. Always."

She lay her head on his chest, listening to the beating of his heart. When she heard it pick up a little faster, she chuckled and looked up at him. "Are you scared or something?"

"Well …" He took a deep breath, and then took her hand. She frowned when he pushed something into her palm.

"What's this?" Looking down, she saw that he put a crumpled napkin in her hand.

"Open it."

Seeing the red ink staining the paper, she chuckled. "Where'd you get this old thing? I thought I'd lost it." She did as he asked and unfurled the napkin in her hand. It definitely was the sketch of the house she made, but she saw something new had been added at the bottom. Scrunching her eyes, she read the words there and gasped. Written in blue ink were the words, "Will you marry me, Amelia?" Slowly, she looked up at him. "Mason?"

"I know it's not a ring," he said sheepishly. "I can't afford one right now, but if you'll have me as your husband, I promise you I'll give you that house one day."

"Yes. Oh, yes." She said it without hesitation, because she already knew she wanted to spend the rest of her life with him.

Mason lifted her up and pressed his lips to hers, and Amelia sighed against him. The warmth of their bond flowed and tightened around them, and she'd never felt more loved and cherished than at that moment. Her bear glowed with happiness, and she felt his animal sigh contentedly. She didn't want the kiss to end, but eventually she pulled away. "Who knew?" she asked.

"Tim and Cassie, of course. And your parents. I asked them for their blessing the first moment we were alone. Your mom had to run to the bathroom to cry."

"Ha!" She remembered that from the other day, when they all had dinner at Rosie's. Cassie said she wanted to grab a coloring book she left in the car and so she went to go get it with her. When they came back, she thought Laura's eyes looked puffy, but her mom had given her an evasive answer when she asked if she was all right.

"Let's go tell everyone," Mason said, after giving her one last kiss.

They walked back in the direction of the cabins but took their time as she wanted to savor the moment some more and keep it to herself. But, as they neared the lake, Amelia felt her bear's hackles raise. Mason stopped suddenly, a soft growl coming from his lips.

"We have company," he said, his eyes glowing. Amelia knew her eyes were lit up too, as her bear was nearing the surface, ready to fight. This was it. The reason she came back. If the intruders harmed a hair on any one of her family's head, she would strike.

Large shadows flew overhead and the winds shook as they passed by. Amelia thought they might have been helicopters or jets, but the loud shrieks and the flapping of wings told her what it was. She looked up. No, those definitely weren't Uncle Hank, Matthew, Jason, or Sybil. "What the hell?" She knew there were other dragons in the world, but they had never ventured into Blackstone.

If Mason was worried, he didn't show it. His Navy SEAL training was kicking in and he was as calm as the cool waters of the lake. "We'll creep up on them and assess the situation." He gripped her hand tight as they moved in.

She followed close behind him as they walked back toward the cabins. As they got nearer, she peered over his shoulder, then frowned at the sight that greeted them. She wasn't sure what she was expecting; a fight in progress maybe, but not this.

Five men were standing in a semicircle in front of Uncle Hank, but he wasn't in a defensive position or even under attack. In fact, he stood confidently, his arms crossed over his chest as he spoke. Matthew and Jason stood behind him, their postures just as assertive as their father's. Everyone—the shifters at least, the humans and the kids were thankfully and noticeably absent—was there behind them, ready to defend their family.

Behind the five men around Uncle Hank were another four men, lined up in a row, though they didn't seem to be trying to defend themselves or in an attack position. In fact, if Amelia didn't know any better, she would say they looked like they were showing off. One of them wore a bright white suit that looked out of place in the middle of the woods.

No one noticed Amelia and Mason as they crept up and joined their family.

"What's going on?" Amelia whispered to Sybil. "Who are those men? Where did they come from?"

Sybil kept her eyes on her father and the other men. "Apparently, they're the Dragon Council."

"Dragon Council? I didn't know you guys had a council."

"Neither did I."

"What do they want?"

Sybil glanced at her father, then back at Amelia. "Some sort of alliance. I don't know. They—the five guys with Dad—just kind of ... appeared out of nowhere. They had some sort of cloaking tech," Sybil explained.

"And the other four?"

"The Dragon Council called them the Alphas of the different clans or something," Sybil continued. "They asked permission to enter our territory, and Dad said yes. They flew in and landed. And—get this—when they shifted back, they had their clothes *on*."

Amelia was shocked but seeing all those men dressed strangely and in clean clothes like they didn't just trudge through the forest, it wasn't an impossibility. Unsure what to say next, she remained silent, but tuned in to listen to the rest of the conversation.

"…And so, Hank Lennox, Blackstone Dragon, we thank you for granting our five Dragon Alphas permission to land in your territory." One of the Dragon Council members, a tall, thin man wearing a silver robe, bowed his head. "And now—"

"Four," Hank interrupted.

"Excuse me?"

"You have four Dragon Alphas," Hank pointed out.

The man turned around, then did a double take. "Where is His Highness?"

The Dragon Alpha in the white suit scoffed. "He must have fallen behind."

"You know those weak little wings of his," another one mocked.

The thin man turned to another council member, a bald man wearing a leather vest and pants. "Where is your prince?"

The man's eyes grew wide. "I-I-I don't … I mean …" He took a handkerchief from his pocket and wiped his forehead. "Maybe he—"

A loud whooshing sound broke through the air. It sounded like—waves? Very big waves, it seemed like.

Everyone turned their heads toward the lake as the water began to rise and rush up. Something very large was moving in the lake, churning the water. Someone gasped audibly when an enormous winged creature leapt up and flew into the air. It was probably as large as Uncle Hank in dragon form, but it had a long body covered with blue and green scales, thin, bat-like wings, and a tail with a fin. The creature stayed airborne for a few more seconds, then dove back into the water.

"What the hell is that?" Mason said. "A snake?"

"A dragon," Sybil said.

The water went quiet and the air was still. Suddenly, a figure rose out of the water. A tall, hulking man began walking up the shore. He was wearing only leather pants and his arms were covered with tattoos that looked like scales. He looked confident and self-assured as he strode toward them, as if he were walking down a fashion runway, not out of a lake.

"Finally," one of the dragon council members said.

The bald man cleared his throat and stepped forward. "May I present, His Royal Highness, Prince Aleksei of the Northern Isles, Jarl of Svalterheim, Dragon Protector of the —" He let out an undignified squeak as the prince pushed him aside. "Your Highness? Where are you going?"

But Prince Aleksei kept walking. He strode past Hank, Matthew, Jason, and the Dragon Council. Amelia's bear rose up in a defensive position and she felt Mason's polar bear do the same as the dragon shifter came closer. Prince Aleksei didn't pay attention to them. In fact, he didn't look at anyone else. His gaze was fixed on one thing—or rather person: Sybil.

"Hello, *mate*." His smile was almost feral when the words came out of his mouth.

Mason put his arm protectively around Amelia and leaned down close to her ear. "What the heck is going on?"

Amelia looked over to her friend. Sybil's face was inscrutable and her body remained frozen to the spot. "It looks like things are about to get interesting in Blackstone." This probably wasn't what the she-dragon had in mind when she'd pined for mate. But, if her friend could be even half as happy as Amelia was with Mason and Cassie in her life, well, she was ecstatic for what was in store for Sybil.

It's **not** the end!
The story continues in
The Blackstone She-Dragon
Available on Amazon

Want to read a (**hot, sexy and explicit**) extended scene from this book?

Sign up for my newsletter here:
http://aliciamontgomeryauthor.com/mailing-list/

You'll get access to ALL the bonus materials from all my books and my **FREE** novella **The Last Blackstone Dragon.**

PREVIEW: THE BLACKSTONE SHE-DRAGON

UNEDITED, RAW, AND SUBJECT TO CHANGE

Sybil Lennox's eyes fluttered open as she heard her alarm clock make its familiar *ring-ding-ding sound*. She reached over to her bedside table and turned it off.

"*Hmmm* …." She sighed audibly as she sat up and stretched her arms over her head. *What a strange dream.* She rubbed the sleep from her eyes some more. Her dream was … she shook her head. She couldn't remember the details, but she remembered feeling *really* good. Like she was floating in a body of warm water.

Her inner dragon agreed. Whatever the dream was, it had been amazing. The creature inside her was content to just laze around in bed, but Sybil was not going to lie down and do nothing this weekend.

I'm so looking forward to today. After all, it was the last weekend of the summer and they were having the annual Lennox-Walker barbecue at Blackstone Lake.

Sybil glanced over at her clock again. It was eight a.m. on a Saturday, but she didn't mind waking up early. It would give her a chance to clean up her apartment, have a cup of coffee and get ready for the barbecue. She was already half-packed as they would be at Blackstone Lake all weekend. It was going to be so much fun, and she was looking forward to spending time with her parents, brothers, and the rest of the family.

She hummed to herself cheerfully as she got showered, dressed in her favorite bathing suit and sundress, and finished packing. By the time she heard the knock on the door, she had just put her three bottles of sunscreen into her bag and zipped it closed.

"Auntie Sybil!" Grayson Mills-Lennox greeted when she opened the door. The five-year-old boy raised his chubby arms up at her, and she obliged by picking him up.

"Hey, Squirt." The scent of bear cub filled her nostrils, and her inner dragon glowed with happiness as it recognized the child. Sybil's animal was especially protective over children, and probably one of the main reasons she decided to be a child welfare advocate. "Ready for the lake?"

"Oh boy, am I ever!"

"Grayson," Georgina, Grayson's mother and Sybil's brother's wife, warned. "You're getting too heavy to be carried like that."

"Aww, Mommy, Auntie Sybil can take me. She's strong, like Papa and Pop-pop."

Sybil laughed. True, as a dragon shifter, she did have enhanced strength, even in human form, which was why she was alway extra careful. "You're growing real big, Grayson." She put him down. "How much mac and cheese have you been eating?"

"Lots!" the boy said proudly.

"We should get going," Georgina said. "Luke is waiting for us outside."

"I'm all ready," Sybil proclaimed. "Are you excited for the weekend?"

"Oh boy, I am. Papa said that we're going to go swimming, and then have barbecue and ..."

Sybil let the boy ramble on as she locked her door and then followed mother and son down to the first floor where Luke's shiny new truck was waiting in the driveway of her apartment complex. She opened the rear passenger door and helped Grayson inside before climbing in.

"Hey Luke." She squeezed his shoulder as she moved into the back seat.

"Sybbie," he greeted back using his favorite childhood nickname. "Did you lock your door?

She rolled her eyes as she strapped Grayson into his car seat. "Yes."

"And you have the timers on your lights?"

"Uh-huh." She patted Grayson on the head, then put her own seatbelt on.

"And you changed the batteries on your smoke detector?"

"Seriously? I'm a dragon, remember?"

Luke's tawny gold eyes stared back at her, dead serious. "Which is why I'm asking. Do you remember when you were eight and you—"

"Shush! That was years ago." She put her hand up. "Fine. Yes, *mom*," she said in a sarcastic tone. "I changed the batteries last week."

"Good." He nodded and turned to his mate. "Ready?" Georgina nodded and Luke put the truck in gear, then drove out to the main road.

Georgina glanced back at Sybil. "You know he's like this because he cares about you right?"

"And because you live in a dodgy neighborhood," Luke added, looking at her from the rearview mirror.

"It is not dodgy," she said defensively. "It's quaint."

"It's dodgy," Luke insisted.

Sybil huffed. "It's near work, which means I save on gas, plus it's what I can afford on my salary." Her apartment complex was located in the less-affluent part of Blackstone, but it was also accessible to the highway that led to the next town. Although the Child Welfare Service Office was located in Blackstone, her division actually served the entire county and most of her cases had her traveling into the surrounding towns.

"You could live at the castle," Luke pointed out.

"So could you," she shot back. Although Luke grunted and turned his attention back to the road, she saw the smile at the corner of her lips. Her brother had always told her how proud he was that she wanted to make her own way in life.

"He just wants you to be happy and safe," Georgina said. "Right, Luke?"

"You need someone to take care of you," Luke said.

"Excuse me?" Sybil said, trying not to raise her voice.

"You know what I mean."

Sybil sat back and crossed her arms over her chest. "You, Jason, and Matthew spent most of my teen years scaring off any boy who came near me, and *now* you're complaining that I don't have a boyfriend?"

"I don't want just *any* boyfriend for you," Luke grumbled. "You should have someone who will respect you and treat you right. Then *maybe*, I might stop worrying about you."

"Now you sound like a nosy old lady, *grandma*." Sybil pouted.

It wasn't that she didn't like guys or wanted to be single

the rest of her life. She didn't even think she was bad looking; she was on the petite side, which meant every guy she met was taller than her; she'd been told she was pretty, with her heart-shaped face, dark lashes, and gray eyes; plus she was sure guys stared at her double-D boobs and her shapely butt all the time.

No, the problem wasn't with this body; it was the *other* body. Her dragon was just too strong and powerful for most of the shifter men in town. Growing up, all the boys in her high school had been terrified of her dragon. She felt their animals cower in fear, even though she'd learned to control her dragon since she was a child. Plus, it didn't help that she was the only daughter of the richest man in town, who practically owned Blackstone. While all the girls her age were experiencing their firsts—first dates, first kisses, first boyfriends, first, *ahem*, times—she had been left in the corner like the veggie dish at a potluck. And by the time she went off to college, she simply had lost hope and interest in boyfriends.

Still, it didn't mean she wasn't open to the possibility. And, if she were honest with herself, she was envious of her family and friends. Everyone had already paired off, finding their mates, while she was left alone again. Even Kate—who swore off relationships—found her mate in Petros. What she wouldn't give to even have a decent date with a nice guy. Just something *normal*.

Georgina sensed the growing tension and cleared her throat. "So, it's still about an hour to the lake. Why don't we play a game. Grayson?"

"Oooh! How about *I Spy*?"

Sybil put all thoughts of boys, boyfriends, and mates aside. "Why don't I go first?" She grinned at Grayson. "I spy with my my little eye …."

PREVIEW: THE BLACKSTONE SHE-DRAGON

After their huge barbecue lunch, the whole Lennox-Walker clan decided it was time for a dip in the lake. Sybil was sitting on the shore, content to watch everyone have fun. Jason, Christina, Petros, and Kate were all playing chicken fight, the girls on their respective mates' shoulders as they tried to push each other over. Matthew and Catherine were lazing on their inflatable tubes, while Luke was teaching Grayson how to swim. Meanwhile, Cassie Grimes was riding on the back of her great-uncle Tim, who was in polar bear form. Cassie's dad, Mason and his mate, Amelia Walker, were sitting on the dock that stretched out from the shore. Laura, Amelia's mom, came over and spoke with them, and when she left, the couple stood up and walked toward the woods.

She was glad Amelia was back, and also, back with her mate. They had broken up a couple of years ago, but when Mason moved to town, they had reunited. Sybil knew part of the story, and she had been there when Amelia had been inconsolable in the wake of the breakup.

Sybil was also the social worker who had checked up on Cassie when she came to Blackstone after an emergency removal from Mason's ex-wife's custody. She could have been vindictive, since Mason broke one of her best friends' heart, but she was a professional. Besides, she'd read Cassie's case file; not only had the young girl been abandoned by her mom, but Mason wasn't even her biological father. Yet he stepped up and took care of her like she was his own. Sybil had to give him props for that.

"Everything okay, Princess?" Her father plopped down on the sand next to Sybil and put an arm around her.

"Hey Dad." She leaned her head on his shoulder. "Yeah, I'm good. You?"

"Doing great, now that I'm here with all of you." He flashed her a smile, the corners of his eyes crinkling. "Are you sure you're okay?"

She laughed. "I'm fine."

"Work's good?"

"Yeah, same old, same old." Her work was never boring, that was for sure, and some days, it was heartbreaking and exhausting. But, seeing the kids smile made it all worth it, especially with what they went through. "I just—Dad?"

Hank's body stiffened and his eyes began to glow. Sybil could feel his inner dragon stand at attention, and her own animal mirrored its sire. The hairs on the back of her stood up, and her skin crawled. *Danger.*

Her father stood up, grabbed her elbow, and pulled her up. The tension in the air was palpable. She looked around her. Matthew, Jason, and everyone else who had been swimming were walking up to the shore. When Hank's head whipped around, she saw what had sent all their senses on alert.

There were five men standing there, right in front of Uncle James' cabin. Now, Sybil was a hundred percent sure they had not been there a second ago, nor had she sensed their approach. In fact, it was like they had just appeared out of thin air.

Hank's jaw set. "The kids. And the women—"

"Christina's taking them inside," Jason said as he came closer.

"Sybil, go with them," Matthew ordered.

"What?" She glanced back at the men, who had not moved an inch. "No way." She looked around her. Luke, Uncle James, Tim, Petros, Kate, and Ben were coming towards them. "I'm one of you, remember?" Her dragon uncoiled inside her, ready to protect her loved ones.

"If they need help—"

"Then I'll fly them off in a sec," Sybil said. "But I'm staying here."

"They're coming," Jason warned.

Hank turned to face the intruders, putting himself between them and his family. Matthew and Jason stood behind him, while the rest spread out behind the trio, flanking all sides.

The five men walked toward them with deliberate steps. As they came closer, Sybil's shifter instincts went into overdrive.

Dragons.

Five dragons had landed in Blackstone. *But why?* Sybil knew of the existence of other dragons in the world, but, like the Lennoxes, most kept a low profile. Her father and brothers never gave out interviews or allowed outsiders into their lives. As Riva had explained when they were teenagers, the Lennox Corp. Public Relations Department's main function was to keep them *out* of the public eye.

Of course, she couldn't help herself: out of curiosity, she'd done a Google search for other dragon shifters, but found very little information. There was a mention of a dragon in Chicago who lived in the tallest building in the world, but there was not much else; it was like the existence of dragons had been scrubbed from the World Wide Web and the greater world in general.

"You will not take another step," Hank said. His tone was calm, but the presence of his dominant dragon was unmistakeable.

The five men stopped in their tracks. Sybil's eyes

narrowed at them. Each one of them wore different clothing, but they were definitely all dragons, though she sensed something was different about each of them. *But what?*

"Greetings, Henry Lennox, Blackstone Dragon." The man in the middle, a tall, thin man wearing silver robes said. He had a pleasant voice with a slight accent Sybil couldn't place. English? Irish?

"Who are you and what do you want?" came Hank's reply.

Another man—this one short and stocky and wore an immaculate white suit—spoke next. "We are the Dragon Council."

"Dragon Council?" Hank echoed. "I've never heard of you."

"Of course not," White Suit said, his aristocratic voice almost a sneer. "Your ancestor, Anastasia Lennox got your clan banished from the Dragon Alliance when she defied dragon law and *mated*," the disdain in his voice was evident, "with a common shifter."

Sybil bit her lip to stop her gasp, but beside her, she could feel Uncle James and Ben tense. She didn't blame them, of course. He was talking about their ancestor, Silas Walker, a bear shifter who had married Anastasia Lennox.

"Caesar, please," Silver Robe interrupted. "That's all in the past, right? Does it matter?"

"What matters is why you're here. On my mountain," Hank said, his arms crossing over his chest. "How the hell did you sneak up on us and what do you want?"

"We Cloaked, of course," Silver Robe replied matter-of-factly. "Have you never Cloaked before?"

Caesar clucked his tongue and turned to Silver Robe. "See, Balfour? I told you, we don't even know how they've regressed, being away from other dragons."

Balfour's eyes flashed silver. "*Please*, Caesar." He turned back to Hank. "Kindly excuse us. As Dragon Council, we put everything to a vote and unfortunately, my compatriot lost this one."

Hank looked at the men impatiently. "Will one of you just please tell me what's going on?"

"Since you are apparently unaware of the events of the past century or two, let me start from the beginning." Balfour cleared his throat. "A few thousand years ago, dragon shifters lived peacefully with humans and all other shifters; however, through the centuries, humans began to hunt us down and thus, those of us that remained formed the Dragon Alliance. Each clan sends one representative to the Dragon Council, who then creates and enforces Dragon Laws. These laws are meant to keep us safe and ensure the survival of our species." He paused. "When, uh, your ancestor, Anastasia Lennox broke dragon law, the Lennoxes were banished from the Dragon Alliance as punishment."

"Their lands and titles were taken, as were their treasure hoards, and they were left to fend for themselves without the protection of the Alliance," Caesar added. "That is what happens when you break dragon law."

"I think we've been doing well for ourselves," Hank said with a raised brow. Behind him, Jason and Matthew nodded in agreement. "So, you kicked us out of your little club. What the hell are you doing here then?"

Balfour' face turned grave. "There are people—humans—out there who want to destroy us." He looked at the other shifters. "All of us. I know you've already encountered them and that they tried to destroy your town."

"The Organization," Jason said, his hands curling into fists into his sides. The anti-shifter group had tried to blow up the entire town of Blackstone a few months ago.

Balfour nodded. "They call themselves The Knights of Aristaeum. Few know who they are. They were named after a wizard who sought to destroy all shifters."

"Wizards?" Matthew asked.

"Yes. Humans used to know how to wield magic, but they lost the ability over time. It's a long story, but basically, this secret society has existed for the past three centuries, and their main goal is to destroy all shifters."

"Then what do you want with us?" Hank asked.

Balfour looked around uneasily at the other men behind him. Caesar frowned, but nodded. "We seek an alliance with you. And invite you to once again join The Dragon Council."

"And why would we do that?" Matthew said.

"Because The Knights of Aristaeum will destroy us all," Caesar stated matter-of-factly. "All shifters of all kinds. And they already have the means to do it. A magical weapon."

"What?" Hank's voice raised. "What are you talking about?"

Balfour looked around apprehensively. "Blackstone Dragon, before we go any further, we must ask that you meet with the Dragon Alphas."

"All right, I'll bite," Hank sighed. "Dragon Alphas?"

"They are the leaders of the various dragon clans around the world, and the protectors of their territory and people under them," Balfour explained. "Much like you are the protector of Blackstone. If you grant them permission to land in your territory, then we can sit down and talk about how we will stop The Knights."

"I think the idea has merit," Jason said.

"But, can we trust them?" Matthew interjected.

Hank seemed to consider his sons' words. "How do we know this isn't some trap?"

"What?" Caesar scoffed. "What would we have to gain from trapping or betraying you? We are dragons, just like you."

"We don't exactly know you," Hank pointed out. "You show up here and then spout all this bullshit and we're just supposed to believe you?"

Caesar looked offended, but Balfour spoke up. "We swear to you, on the grave of our ancestors, that we only speak the truth. Besides, you know how territorial dragons can be. The moment you tell us to leave, we will be compelled to do so. It is our nature."

Hank huffed. "All right. Tell them they can come. But none of this Cloaking bullshit. They wanna come here? They better show themselves to me."

"Of course." Balfour bowed. "Thank you." He looked back at the other members of the council. "Please, call your Alphas."

Sybil wasn't sure what she was expecting when Balfour told the other dragons to "call" their alphas—maybe take out their phones and text message?—but certainly, she didn't think they would all just close their eyes and go perfectly still. *What the heck—*

A strange sensation passed over her, and there was a force in the air she couldn't describe—like electricity crackling. It filled the atmosphere around them, threatening to spark and explode at any moment. Then, they all looked up.

The sounds of the beating of wings filled the air. The brightness of the sun prevented Sybil from getting a better look, but she could four large shadows overhead. Each one looked different—one of them had two legs instead of four limbs, another had scales like uneven rock—but from the way her own animal reacted, she knew they were all dragons.

One by one, they swooped down, transforming smoothly

into they human forms. Sybil was taken aback when she realized that they were all wearing *clothes*. When shifters changed into their animals, their clothes didn't shift with them. She herself tended to remove her clothes and leave them somewhere safe or take them with her, clutched in her claws. But these dragons didn't need to do that. *Huh.*

All four stood behind the dragon council, their stances confident. It was obvious why they were the Alphas. Power radiated from each of them like a beacon. And, much to her chagrin, all of their eyes zeroed in on *her.*

Sybil gulped. But she had to admit, she was curious, too. She had never met a dragon she wasn't related to. And *attractive* ones.

Like most shifters, they were all tall, with muscular bodies, and good-looking in their own individual ways. The one with icy blue eyes and white blond hair stared at her with such intensity she thought his gaze would burn a hole right through her. The other three looked at her curiously, as if trying to catch her eye.

Her own inner dragon, on the other hand, scoffed and swished its tail in disdain, not caring for their attention. *Choosy much?* she huffed at the creature. But then again, her dragon had never shown interest in any male, shifter or not.

"Ahem." Caesar cleared his throat and all the Alphas snapped back their attention to the Council.

"What's going on? Who are those men? Where did they come from?" Amelia asked.

Sybil startled, not realizing that she and Mason had come back from their walk. "Apparently, they're the Dragon Council."

"Dragon Council? I didn't know you guys had a council."

"Neither did I."

"What do they want?"

That was the million dollar question. "Some sort of alliance. I don't know. They—the five guys with Dad—just kind of ... appeared out of nowhere. They had some sort of cloaking tech," Sybil explained.

Amelia pointed her chin at the Alphas. "And the other four?"

"The Dragon Council called them the Alphas of the the different clans or something. They asked permission to come in our territory, and Dad said yes. They flew in and landed. And—get this—when they shifted back, they had their clothes on." Sybil turned her attention back to the council.

"....And so, Hank Lennox, Blackstone Dragon, we thank you for granting our five Dragon Alphas permission to land into our territory." Balfour bowed his head. "And now—"

"Four," Hank interrupted.

"Excuse me?"

"You have *four* Dragon Alphas."

Hmmm. Sybil looked around. Yes, there were definitely only four Alphas.

Balfour did a double-take. "Where is His Highness?"

The other Dragon Alphas spoke, and Sybil couldn't hear them, it looked like they didn't know or care, judging from their body language.

Balfour turned to another man from the council. "Dmitri, where is your prince?"

"I-I-I don't ... I mean ...." Dmitri wiped his balding, sweaty head with a handkerchief. "Maybe he—"

The sound of water rushing made everyone freeze. The din was almost deafening and whatever was making it sounded very big. A humungous wave cut through the waters of the lake and Sybil let out a gasp as something burst out from the water.

Oh.

Sybil's inner dragon perked up when the winged creature flew up in the air. It was large, about fifty feet long and covered in beautiful, shimmering blue-green scales. Its bat-like wings were long and delicate, but allowed it to propel through the air. It didn't have any other limbs, but its back was spiked with dorsal fins, and its tail was shaped like the fluke of a dolphin, but matched the rest of its body and wings. As quickly as it rose up, it dove back into the water.

"What the hell is that?" Mason said. "A snake?"

"A dragon." Sybil's throat went dry.

The air felt thick, and for a moment, Sybil couldn't breathe. A figure rose from the water and as soon as her eyes landed on it, she felt the air rush back into her lungs.

A man began to walk out of the water, shaking droplets out of his long, light brown hair . A *very* large man, even by shifter standards. He was tall, probably six-and-a-half feet, with broad shoulders that seemed as wide. His muscled arms were covered with tattoos that resembled scales, made obvious because he only wore leather pants and no shirt, which also showed off a sculpted chest, a cut set of eight-pack abs, and the deep V cut on his hips. He looked like he spent hours at the gym, but not in a gross way like those pro body-builders on TV.

As he strode out of the lake, Sybil felt the beating of wings inside her as her inner dragon flittered excitedly. *Flittered?* That was strange. It had never done that before.

"Finally," Caesar said dryly.

Dmitri took a step forward. "Ahem. May I present, His Royal Highness, Prince Aleksei of the Northern Isles, Jarl of

Svalterheim, Dragon Protector of the—Eeek!" He nearly tumbled over when he was pushed aside.

Prince Aleksei didn't acknowledge the presence of the other Alphas, the Council, or even Hank Lennox. Instead, he moved forward with purpose. Sybil glanced around, wondering where he was going. And then she realized where he was headed.

Oh. Her inner dragon began to get even more excited, fluttering around inside her, its wings beating a mile a minute. Or was that her heartbeat?

He stopped in front of her, and his dark green eyes shifted colors as they stared down. Sybil's inner dragon went still.

"Hello, *mate.*"

Mine. Mate.

Sybil nearly jumped out of her skin at the loudness of her dragon's voice. This was her *mate?*

The Blackstone She-Dragon
Available now on Amazon

ABOUT THE AUTHOR

Alicia Montgomery has always dreamed of becoming a romance novel writer. She started writing down her stories in now long-forgotten diaries and notebooks, never thinking that her dream would come true. After taking the well-worn path to a stable career, she is now plunging into the world of self-publishing.

facebook.com/aliciamontgomeryauthor
twitter.com/amontromance
bookbub.com/authors/alicia-montgomery

Printed in Dunstable, United Kingdom